KAYLA DARGIN

Paperback ISBN: 978-1-63616-035-1

eBook ISBN: 978-1-63616-036-8

Published by Opportune Independent Publishing Company

For permission requests, write to the publisher, addressed "Attention: Permissions Coordinator" to the address below.

Email: Info@opportunepublishing.com

Address: 113 N. Live Oak Street
Houston, TX 77003

Table of Contents

Introduction

On November 25, 1993, Thanksgiving Day another African American girl was added to the population. I'm pretty sure she was eager to stretch and get out of that crowded place. Also, to make faces of the voices she heard while in her mother's womb. Not knowing the world, she would face would put her right back in that tight crowed space. Having no clue about parenthood her parents were only babies having a baby. Her mother was 15 and her father was 14.

A family that was broken before it began. Drugs, jail, heartache, streets, fear, depression, anxiety, insecurity, and stress were only months away from entering that baby girl's life and she had no clue of what it would turn her into. Her grandmother always said the same thing that a make you laugh would make you cry. Kay's family wasn't perfect, but it was their mistakes, struggles, and troubles that made her the woman she became.

Her granny made sure to install that ol' skool loving in Kay's soul. When she wasn't sitting outside with her and Jezzy smoking her candy cigarettes, drinking her coffee, and hitting either two natural lights, they were filling her mind and soul with ol' skool music. Otis Redding, Smokey Robinson, Al Green, Sir Charles, The Commodores, Bobby Womack, Teddy Pendergrass,

Wilson Meadows, Johnnie Taylor, Tyrone Davis, David Brinston, and any artist from the '70s to '80s. Kay would sing them word for word like she herself had been through hurt and pain.

This story isn't for people to feel pity or even bash Kay's family. This story is simply a message to all the young women in the world with a background similar or worse. Let this be guarding tool through those rough days and late nights.

Chapter One
Wakeup

At the age of 26, I now sit with the wisdom from all of the situations and changes I've been through. When you are born in this world you don't get a to-do list or how-to-do list. You basically grow through whatever you go through. Many times, I questioned why me, why I wasn't born with a silver spoon, and just basically why me. As I grew through all of the changes and messed-up situations, it taught me how not to touch that hot stove again. It also taught me that if you can't learn and grow from your mistakes you will repeatedly go through them until you learn. The truth is you will be hurt by family, friends, and peers, but it's how you react that determines your karma. Revenge is only a darker side of you that acts on emotions. Emotions can be a good thing but can also be the very thing that holds you back.

Prior to now, I was hungry for freedom, knowledge, success, and emotional relief. I found myself meditating more, training myself to utilize my tools and skills, and simply finding myself. The truth is that I noticed that I never really loved myself because if I did, I would have been happy a long time ago. I had been miserable for a long time holding my head down and steady running from my mistakes, instead of embracing them.

I remember like it was yesterday–at the age of 24, I met a man, "Trewf", that confirmed my awareness and ability. Trewf literally turned a light on in my head and shined a light on who I really was. I was so amazed at the type of Black male figure he was. He was very self-discipline. He taught me the number one rule that I had been missing for so long not all black men are the same. He wasn't ordinally, like most of our Black men— lost running around like dogs in heat, with the pink thing hanging out from their penises. Whenever I had questions or needed clarification he was there.

From that point on, I was reading more, writing down my thoughts, and feeling like I could conquer the world. He was the support that I had been missing from my adolescent years. I grew up with both of my parents in and out of jail. They spent more time in the streets than raising and teaching me things. My grandmother took me in when she had eight kids of her own and I'll forever be grateful and happy for that. If it wasn't for her, I wouldn't be here sharing my story with you.

Of course, being a young Black woman not knowing who I was, or what to stand for and believe in caused me to fall and bump my head multiple times. There were many days I contemplated committing suicide. I bet you're questioning or asking, "Dang, what could've caused that."

Well, here's the answer: At the age of 10, I notice I was less fortunate than the other kids. I envied those that did have and always stared with jealousy in my eyes when I saw another little girl with more fortunate things. Especially the ones that had both a father and mother in their lives. My grandmother must have taken notice of my behavior because then the teaching begins. Her words were, "Baby treat others how you want to be treated. Don't ever do on to others that you wouldn't want to be done to you."

At the time, I didn't understand, and it went completely over my head. Even though she would tell me how sweet and beautiful I was, I still couldn't see it when I looked in the mirror. I didn't know what I was here for or who I was. Not knowing who you are is the biggest downfall a human could ever face. When you go through that stage of the unknown, anybody can label or put a thought of who they think you are in your mind and heart.

Things like ugly, black, skinny, poor, hoe, bitch, slut, etc., had defined me at an early age. Because of not knowing who I was at the time. When you have the proper tools and guidance, the unknown is good/high qualities to you. The clothes, shoes, popularity, beauty, and a stable house were what separated me from the other girls. Well, at least that's what I thought at the time. I questioned and beat myself up constantly for 10 years - Why I couldn't have what they had? Why have none of the boys wanted to pick me to be their girlfriend or send me letters? Was I that unpretty? I questioned. Having a lost soul is a painful enduring.

Thanksgiving Day, I was brought into this world. I was Innocent, not knowing what to expect. Not knowing that I was born into poverty, but also that my parents were only fifteen and sixteen at the time they had me. Babies having a baby. My father was a thug, and my momma was just moving fast before her time. How could they raise a baby? Many questioned, but my Momo Cindy (my maternal grandmother) knew from the start that she wasn't allowing my momma to raise me or let my daddy be around me. My grandmother despised my daddy so much for being a street thug that she wanted Black to be my daddy.

Even when my daddy told her that he knew I was

his baby, my grandmother still went against it. All she knew was that my daddy's momma was on drugs and their house was a crack house. She didn't care how much my Momo Wanda (paternal grandmother) wanted to be a part of my life and how much she cried that she couldn't. In her head and heart, she was protecting me from seeing all the craziness that went on over there.

My few days after being welcome home turned into a drama scene quick. After my momma took me from my grandmother house. My Momo Cindy went biolistic and went over to get me. D'wana, my daddy sister, opened the door and Cindy burst into my father's mother house yelling "I'm here to get my damn grand baby out this crack house right now."

D'wana ran to wake her brother and my mother up. Bird and Vera was sound asleep not knowing Vera's mother were on the urge of pulling a kick door for her grandchild. That she knew from the day one was hers. Her bug eyes and chocolate brown skin made Cindy fall in love at first sight. Vera jumped up and ran to the front room to spot not only Cindy was there, but Jezzy was there too. Aww shit she thought these two are up to no good. Cindy then screamed "Vera where in the hell is my baby?"

Vera then replied, "Aww momma she's in the bed with her grandmother."

Jezzy then said, "Go get her right damn now nobody told you to take her damn it."

Vera said, "She's my baby damn."

All the commotion woke Bird up. When Cindy seen him, her blood boiled. "You drug dealer no life thug where my grand baby?" she asked.

Vera screamed "Momma don't talk to him like that!"

Bird smiled a cool and collective smile and said, "Nah it's cool look she's in that room right there" while pointing to his momma room.

Cindy and Jeezy busted in the room. Wanda was laying naked in the bed with me. Cindy went mad "You nasty mother fucker give me my grandbaby this instant!"

Dora looked up wiping the sleep out of her eyes scanned both women face like what the hell is going on. Wanda and Bird was now in the doorway trying to calm the women down. Vera mind was racing she knew if Wanda didn't hand the baby over that instant, it would start a fist fight. She also knew Cindy best friend Jezzy was riding for Cindy all day. They would jump Dora and she knew it. Wanda finally saw what was going on and said, "Mother fuckers this my grandbaby too."

Cindy yelled back "Fuck no it's not that's Black baby.

Bird said, "Momma just give her to Ms. Cindy."

"Yeah, that's right you hoodlum tell your nasty momma release her now!" Cindy yelled.

As Cindy went to grab me off the bed Dora grab me too. Jezzy then stepped closer and said, "Now you listen to me unloose that baby this second."

Lannie stepped in between Jezzy and Wanda because now Jezzy wasn't high yellow anymore she was beck red. Jezzy was a high yellow about 4'3" feisty woman that people knew better than to fuck with. Lannie said "Dora please just give my momma Kay please."

This was Cindy and Dora first grand baby. Dora was about 5'1 reddish fine little something. All the men wanted her, and you can bet they paid just to touch her. Now Cindy was the opposite real classy, long hair, caramel complexion with high cheek bones. Would sweep a man off his feet with her calm voice and loving spirit. Let's not forget knew how to throw down in the kitchen. Talking about character the spitting image of big momma off "Soul Food".

Bird who now saw it was getting out of hand grabbed Kay and gave her to Cindy. Wanda began to cry "No Bird, that's our baby too man, she won't know us!"

Cindy gave a look that if it could kill Dora would be dead and said, "That is not his baby this baby is for Black."

Dora cried even louder. Bird said, "Mrs. Cindy take Kay but that's my baby."

Bird was very humbled, respectful, and always kept it 100 and some. He was about 5'8 dark complexion figure of basketball player with a box afro. Yes, he was a thug every bone in his body was gangster, but he would never disrespect his elders. Bird opened the door to let Jezzy and Cindy out. Cindy gently turned to Vera and said, "You can stay in this crack house but not my baby."

Bird watched as both ladies got into the car to make sure they made it in safely. Once they drove off, he blew a kiss towards the car and said daddy loves you baby girl. He didn't feel any type of way by what Cindy said he knew he had to keep his sisters fed. His momma was a smoker, and their daddy were long gone. So, he had to step up at an early age and handle business. He wasn't proud of it but that's what he was forced to do. He walked in the room put on his CD and put his favorite sound on Tupac "White man world."

He turned to Lannie and said, "I know that's my baby."

Lannie was about 4'5 dark skin, coke bottle shaped, plus bow-legged made all the men stop what they were doing were doing when she passed by. Real foxy lady. She said, "I know she is too."

My daddy got into some trouble and went to jail for a very long time so my Momo Wanda was just trying to be there because she knew my daddy couldn't. I didn't remember my father at all, so it was easy for me to think

Maxwell (the singer) was my daddy when I saw him on BET. All I remembered about my daddy was that he had an afro the last time I saw him, which is why I thought Maxwell was my father.

Lannie tried her best to be consistent with letters and pictures. After the months passed by, she found herself messing around with other men breaking the loyalty and trust with my father. In the streets men barely had women that would be loyal and wait on their arrival. They would always jump ship and end up with a familiar face or even a home boy. That just was the way the game was played.

They just couldn't fight the urge of wanting a man next to them. They had given Bird 5 years so Lannie knew he wouldn't be home no time soon. I wasn't getting any younger I was steady growing and very smart for my age. I could hold a full conversation at the age of 2 and if you let Cindy tell it I was born walking. G.A., my Momo Cindy husband, would pump me up with nothing but the candy and had me bouncing off the wall full of energy. I was very spoiled behind him. Everywhere he went, I was on his hip. G.A. didn't mind one bit because he loved bragging on his beautiful granddaughter. Even Lex, the family dog, who was also was growing old loved and protected her.

They were more like sisters than anything else. I had no one else to play with besides Lex. Up until I got to know Ms. Lady that moved next door. I didn't know her name, so I just called her Ms. Lady. Ms. Lady sold cold cups and she was always given me one. I became very familiar with her and her son Drew. I talked about them so much until Cindy wanted to know who was given her grandbaby cold cups over the fence. She went meet Ms. Lady herself to judge rather I should be taking stuff from her or not. Her and Cindy became acquainted with one another to the point I would go and chill by Ms. Lady house when I wanted to. One day after leaving Ms. Lady house I noticed my Momo cooking our food outside in the ground. My innocent mind not knowing the reason for it was because the lights were out. Instead, I thought it was cool and went sit by my Momo and kept her company. Cindy was hurting inside but felt joyful when I came sit by her and helped her cook. Lex came snuggle under me as well. Everyone was humbled and calm until J-Reed notice his rabbit was gone. He started screaming "I'm kill him I swear."

G.A. had done kilt his rabbit to cook it and he knew it. Cindy went to sooth J-Reed down, but he wasn't having it. He stormed off down the street without a care in the world. Cindy fussed at G.A. but he didn't care he thought he didn't owe anyone an explanation he was the daddy.

Bob came into the house one day after school with a friend name Reggie. As little and young as I was had done fell in love with him. I would follow him all around the house. Bob noticed and asked Reggie "What the hell have you done to my niece man?"

Reggie busted out laughing I don't know man. Cindy had to stay up many nights hearing my story about Reggie and I had to get a house and pay bills, it cracked Cindy up because what in the world did, I know about bills and a house. She told me I was an old soul and had been here before. I was very smart and advance. Everyone in the house knew that except for Vera who wasn't around much.

The all thought it was cute. Well, that's at least up until the day I told the cops that Uncle B-Rock had the weed. They all were in aww even the cop, but they couldn't do nothing but laugh at me. I was banded from the outhouse in the back because I would always go tell my Momo one was smoking when it was all of them. Latifah had become best friends with Tiff who would come by the house all the time so they can go in the outhouse and smoke that weed. It would be a whole group of them hanging out and every time they let me in, I would tell Cindy everything I heard and saw. They wanted to kill me. Vera had got so fed up with it she went to wipe me, and Lex started growling and stood up to attack her. Cindy heard me crying and went running to see what was wrong. All she could do was tell Lannie put the belt down and leave me alone because Lex was going to attack her. She saw it written all over Lex face and felt it in her bones that Lex wasn't going to stop either. Lex was an Alaskan husky mixed with wolf. Lannie turned to Lex saying, "Lex you really going to bite me?"

Lex stood there and didn't budge or blink. Lannie then saw that Lex wasn't playing she dropped the belt and said fuck it and stormed off. Lex then came check me out to see if I was okay even scanning my body. I hugged Lex which confirm I was okay. We were like peas in the pot. Even when she dropped her puppies nobody could go under the house and touch them without Lex threating to bite them, but she let me climb under the house and go get them. Shocking everybody in the house and damn near scaring Cindy to death. For the simple fact Lex could have turned on me and bite me or even worse kilt me. She fussed at me but took it back because she knew Lex wouldn't harm me ever.

The next few years my last three uncles and myself became close. Well, my Uncle Chuck still had a grudge because when I was born, he wasn't the baby anymore. So, it didn't surprise me when he told my Uncle Snoop, I had got the ratel comb stuck in his duck tail while we were watching Dragon Ball Z. He jumped up and the comb was daggling from his head. He grabbed me and slung me in the other room. I jumped up screaming and went tell my Momo. She stormed in the room telling him he shouldn't have threw me it was just hair. He screamed, "You always taking up for that girl."

It didn't end there I ended up making up my Uncle Chuck, Uncle Snoop, & Bob putting make up on they face and drew on they back with a permanent marker. Boy did they wanted to kill me. My grandmother had to keep me close to her for a few days to protect me from them. My Nanny Mariah use to come take me away every now and then and buy me all kind of fancy clothes and shoes. Her and my Paron had moved to Houston and was doing quite well for they self. I loved it there because she had no kids, and I got all the attention. Especially the rides in her drop top convertible.

Next thing you know Mariah was pregnant and it was a girl I was so excited and happy. When she brought Michelle home, I tried to help by changing her pamper and lotion her down. Boy did I have lotion and baby powder all over. They must have died laughing. A few months later came Poppa. Mariah now had 2 kids. I was no longer the only grandchild even though to my uncles and aunties I was more of their little sister than they niece.

Growing up, my Momo Cindy's house wasn't that different as my Momo Wanda house. They just hide what the grown up did away from the children and it was more of a family house. When we moved from the Trash Pile to Brick Yard our family home turned into a party house. My five uncles and two Aunties had an entourage of friends when they all came together back in those days, they knew how to get together and have fun. Every now and then a fight would break loose, but overall, we all had fun. My cousins and I enjoyed watching the dice games, card games, and even dance lessons from the elders. Every now and then when the house got too crowded and there was too much going on, they would send us out to the front room while the grownups were on the front porch and the den. The ones that played dice, smoked weed too. Sometimes there may have been a little bit of drugging going on. The ones that played cards, drank and got their "Nose a little dirty" were in the den. From early mornings to late nights, our house was lit.

Next thing you know, Latifah was pregnant with Moon. Her baby's father other baby's momma was running Latifah all around the South Side until she finally got enough and let her have it. My Momma even got mace trying to stand up for her during a fight that was supposed to be Latifah in Ina Claire down the street from my momma project. After all the running, she finally got tired and handled her business. Then she ended up letting Big Blessing go and later meeting Luda.

Chapter Two
Sweet Thang-Mary J Blidge

One day, at my grand momma's house, everyone laid down and watched movies like "Soul Food," "The Five Heartbeats," and later "The Temptations." I kept looking at Luda because someone had blackened his eye. It caught my attention because it was my first time ever seeing something like it. My Momo Cindy noticed me staring and said that it wasn't nice to stare. "But Momo, look at his eye," I said.

She ended up shushing me and told me to watch TV.

Next thing you know, Luda started bringing his nephews and nieces around, and there he was.... Luda called him "Quincy." He was so handsome, very quiet, but very bold at the same time. He knew he was the boss and that all of us were going to do what he said. Every time we played anything; he was the one that picked it. His sisters were the closest to my age, so I was happy to finally have someone my age to play with because I was more than three years older than my cousins. We became friends immediately and I became sweet on Quincy. I was too shy to ever say what I wanted to him. I would always just go along with whatever he wanted to play and always was close to him. I had a huge crush!

It was so big that the grownups notice it before he even had a clue that I liked him. We were only five and six then. Oh, but when he did, he learned he now had a cheerleader to cheer him on… literally.

After that, hide and seek then turned into hide and go get it. He would always catch me so he could kiss me when the others weren't looking. We were babies; not knowing what we were doing but knew we liked each other. But when he would get around other people, or should I say girls, he would act like he didn't like me. It seemed the more he acted like that, the more I wanted him. They stayed the whole Summer and I ended up staying the whole Summer by Luda's house because Latifah had moved in with him by then. Quincy's father, Luda's brother, was in jail with a life sentence and had been there for a good bit of time. When they would come to Louisiana from Texas, they would spend the Summer with Zeta, their great grandmother. Quincy would have us all in the gully when I went spend the day over there with them. He was a bad, "yellow bone" and he knew it. So, it didn't take much time for him to end up at White Girl Jody's house next door to his grandmother. It made me so uncomfortable and mad, that I was ready to go and when Luda came to me asking where he was at. I made it known where and that I was ready to go home. How could I have feelings so strong at that age? We were in Kindergarten and Second grade at the time, but I just knew I liked him and had to have him.

**The summer flew by with many memories that year. Right before school was about to start back up Quincy and his siblings had to go back, but they promised they would come back when they could. I was lost without them when they left. Starting Second grade at Southwest Elementary was the same thing I was trying to fit in but always stood out. I wanted to be the class clown just to get the right attention or at least that what type of attention I needed. My momma ended up meeting Red and wanted me to go live with them, so I had to switch schools and go to South Street. I hardly knew anybody, so I was very quiet and never got in trouble there. My teacher loved me. I met Brittany and Green Eye after a few months of being in solitude. I like Green Eye he made me laugh all the time. Even when I didn't feel like laughing. Back at Red's mother house we moved in I was catching hell. I wasn't apart of the family, and I didn't feel like it either.

They always treated me like crap when my mom would go to work. I was ready to go back home to my grandmother. Red use to whip me so much for little, small things and my mom would let him. He used to make me kneel while he slashed me with a belt with full force. Bruising my legs and leaving whelps. I got away in my head by thinking of Quincy and what life would be like when we get older. Soon the whippings got out of hand and ended up venting to Brittany about them during restroom time showing her the bruises. She told our teacher, and our teacher called my grandmother. My grandmother and Paw Paw GA picked me up from school and took me back home. Red was so controlling he had stopped my momma from going to my grandmother.

So, I couldn't tell them. Not only was he whipping on me constantly, but he fought my momma too. I felt so hopeless not being able to protect us both. My grandmother called my mother immediately after coming get me telling her I was to never return there again. You can stay and let him kick your ass if you want, she said. My grandmother kept me at South Street the remainder of the year. Before I knew it Summer was back, and Quincy and Tella was back like they never left. Boy did we have a blast. My father was released from prison that Summer I remember us playing kick ball in the front yard when this car pulled up. I knew the moment I saw his face that he was my daddy. I ran and jumped into his arms. My grandmother house was jumping and everybody that was anybody was there. My daddy stayed for a little then promised me he would be right back before he left. I waited all day and almost all night. He never showed. The next day we got wind that my daddy went back to jail. Talking about crushed my spirit. Quincy was there to take my mind off it in fact this time he stayed behind a little longer after Summer was over. Next thing you know my mother went to jail right behind him.

The love grew stronger for Quincy I wanted a long-term relationship with him, like what I saw when I watched "Love and Basketball" and "The Wood." From my Second-grade year until the 6th grade, even when he wasn't around, he was my boyfriend. Even though he had outside relationships with other girls and even flirted with them when I was around. I was so naïve I bet y'all are wondering how or why you would allow him to do that to you?

The truth is that I fell in love with him the first time I laid eyes on him. I saw a future in us that he didn't see. We came from the same background, and we practically grew up together. Not having my daddy around made me feel incomplete and I just wanted to be loved by the opposite sex. So even though Quincy made me feel stupid, he also made me feel very special when he would hold and kiss on me. He'd tell me sweet things in my ear and made me feel butterflies in my stomach that I never felt before. If only someone would have sat me down and told me that boys and men mature slower than little girl and women, then I may have fought harder to keep our bond.

The middle of my third grade my mother was released from prison my grandmother and pawpaw had to attend anything dealing with parents that year because my parents couldn't make it. My momma ended up going back to Red after saying she wouldn't. This time he asked her to marry him. She said yes of course and boom there I was again leaving my grandmother house to stay with them once again. He promised my grandmother he changed but the only thing changed was his parents gave them a home to live in. I was miserable there the fights still went on and once again he was hitting on me. They got this boy from around the way named Dell to walk me to and from school every morning.

Over time we grew close, and I started to tell him everything. How my step daddy constantly whipped me I couldn't go nowhere, and we didn't have hot water at the time. Red and my mother went back and forth fussing and fighting. Till one day it got so bad I thought he was gone to kill her. I ran to the neighbors and told them to call 911 he's trying to kill my momma. The cops came my uncles and they friends jumped on Red, and my momma left once again saying she wasn't going back. It went on like that for two years in the mix of that my mom got on drugs and had my brother and later my sister MumPatty.

A week or two after my sister was release from the hospital Chad ended up killing Dell right in front of our family house. Right in front of Bob. Dell was like an uncle to me he always was teaching us the new dance moves. He looked like Snoop Dog and wore barrettes on his ponytails. Bob was so much in soak he left the scene with Chad and drove straight to our house. All I remember was having a feeling something wasn't right before the knock came to the door. Bob asked my momma where I was. Chad and Bob were full of blood my momma was in shock screaming, "what happened?" "Chad killed Dell where is Tootie,", the nickname only him and my daddy called me, Bob asked? As I walked out of my room, I heard my momma saying no Bob don't tell her that.

Soon as I hit the porch Bob raced to me and embraced me with a tight hug. "Dell gone Tootie", he said. In the back on him I saw Chad pacing the ground saying I didn't mean to. Something in my bones told me our family would never be the same again blood was shed on our property. Bob in return turned to alcohol to help soothe the pain. Quincy started to come around holidays and Summertime now. Seems like when I was with him all my troubles would melt away. His family was no different than mines. His mother was on drugs, his great grandmother Blanco was like a female drug lord, and his father was doing life. So, I was never embarrassed about my family with him. Drugs and alcohol started to take over my family and slowly we started losing everything we owned. My Momo Cindy, Nanny Maria, Poppa, and Michelle had moved to Lake Charles.

So, holidays weren't the same anymore. My momma eventually got tired of the back and forth with Red and left him saying this time was for good. Six grade year my momma went to the shelter promising to get her life together and my grandmother and the rest returned back to Opelousas. She had been in and out of jail just like my father who was back in jail his self. I went stay to not be apart from my brother and sister. I was back at South Street once again. Boy did I bounce from school over the years. My momma was in AA meeting and Drug court. My godmother Linda was working at the shelter, and she made the time there not feel so bad. I was embarrassed and hide the fact that I stayed there to my classmates. My momma was doing good up until she moved out the shelter and into the house with Ms. Thelma a lady, she met at drug court. Red and my momma started back sneaking around again. At this point they were both felons and it was against the law for them to be together. My momma was working at a furniture store doing good then boom one day we was at Red's momma house and the cops came and took her to jail. Only this time it was Saint Gabriel. My siblings and I went back to stay with my grandmother. Quincy ended up moving to Opelousas and going to the exact same school as me.

Quincy wasn't a virgin anymore and he was having sex, so that's what he wanted. We went to the same school, rode the same bus, and even got off at the same stop—which was his grandmother's house where we were never alone to even try it. His family knew we were sweet on each other, just as well as mines, so they made sure we weren't left alone. Of course, that year and at that age, we tried, but got caught before we could even start. That year, I lost my best friend, his sister Tella, because of one of his flings being so jealous of our relationship. I should have opened my mouth and addresses the lies she told her right then and there, but me being the quiet shy person I was at that time, let it go. Not knowing that she was going to be the realest friend I ever had. His sister and I did everything together; when you saw me, you saw her. But with a blink of an eye, all of that ended two weeks before my sixth-grade year ended. Around graduation time, I knew that everything was about to change, and I was about to say goodbye to my childhood life.

That Summer, my grandmother's trailer was set

on fire. The trailer that she was renting to own was for Quincy's Auntie and she was almost done paying it off, before it went up in flames. My Momo Cindy was so hurt because my graduation dress and pictures were in the trailer during the fire. It was hurtful because she had made sure I had a decent dress and hairstyle because my birth mother was in St. Gabriel at the time. After the fire, we all had to go live with my Uncle Carlton and his wife.

That Summer, I laid in bed all day watching Lifetime movies while everyone else I knew went to the North or South Park pool and skating rink. My grandmother never let me go anywhere and at the time it didn't matter. I made a promise to myself that I would forget about Quincy. My grandmother told me the reason I couldn't let go was because our souls were tied to one another. At the time, I said, "Momo you're crazy."

So, I just went on with my Summer laying around, watching TV, eating, taking baths, and watching more Lifetime movies. My grandmother finally said, "Girl, you're going to turn into a bitter old woman watching that. Go play outside with your cousins and get out of the house," she said.

"You have an old soul, my baby, and you're very gifted. If he can't see that, then he's a fool."

That day, my grandmother must have spoken to my soul because, after that, I began coming out of the room and playing with my little cousins. My cousins, Michelle and Poppa, were like my brother and sister before my momma started having other kids. Our bond was unbreakable. That Summer went by so fast, and my grandmother found another trailer on the Trash Pile before school started.

My daddy had gotten out of jail again and took me to register for Opelousas Jr High School. As we registered for that school year, I noticed that my father couldn't write in cursive. At that time, I didn't understand why education was so important. I was a hard- head that didn't want to listen to any of my elders because of the things I saw them doing. Truth be told, I didn't have a role model growing up. Instead, I had people that I knew I didn't want to be like.

My grandmother was doing the best she could with no support; she managed to keep a roof over her eight kids and their four kids' heads for years. It's funny how we didn't know we were struggling because my grandmother made it to where we saw the good in our situation. Us simply being with one another meant everything to us. Not knowing that we didn't have much is what made those days the best ones we ever had. I didn't grow up with a mother nor father, only my grandmother and I still saw the pure in the world.

When my father got out of jail, my grandmother told him she was tired, and I knew she was. My mother had now three kids ten years after me and my grandmother stepped in to help her before and after St. Gabriel. She always said my mother showed differences between Athena and me because she always kept Mumpatty and Duttie with her.

My father told my grandmother that he would take me to live with him to remove some of the pressure from her. He had just come from spending almost two years in the Parish, where he married Nikki while in jail.

My first year at Opelousas Junior High is when I started gaining self-confidence. I was noticing my beauty but was still insecure. I was still a virgin when I met Dee—a handsome, yellow-boned guy with really good hair. I was in the streets then; All I knew was outside. I started losing sight of school. I quickly went from an honor roll student to the class clown. Yes, I still loved to go to school but not for the good grades or to finish, instead, I went to clown. I got to the point where I was barely passing my classes. Not knowing that I was only stunting my growth and how far I would have gotten if I knew then what I know now. I was never the girly girl type. I was a tomboy more like the girl version of a homie.

Dee shocked me when he told me he took interest in me. Why me? I wondered. He made me feel like I was on top of the world. Making my heart skip a beat when he was near. Making me walk a certain direction just to meet up with him. Of course, my daddy didn't approve of our connection. My father was trying to make up for the ten years he missed out on, so in his mind, I couldn't share any time with a little boy. If only he was there the past ten years to show and tell me how a man should love care and treat me, then. That wouldn't have been happening.

We bumped heads a lot about Dee. I didn't want to hear anything he had to say because it was coming from the man that married the woman that couldn't stand his daughter. Nikki wanted him all for herself and hated the way our bond was. I heard her multiple times telling him he loved me way more than her. How stupid could she be, I thought. This was the very same woman my mom opened her doors to for her to come stay by our house when she had nowhere to go. Fine, I thought, if she doesn't like me then I don't like her. So, for me to stay away from her meant that I had to stay away from my father as well. Truth is, he had spoiled me the few years I did have with him. So naturally, that was the hardest pill a girl could ever have to swallow, leaving my daddy behind and not being around anymore. At the age of fourteen, I ended up losing my virginity, only to find out that he lied about his age and was only eleven years old.

Yes, you read right—eleven! That wasn't the worst part though. The biggest issue was he told his homeboys and one of them told my father.

Why would he go and do such a thing, I questioned? Did he not know my father would try to kill him, literally? Which lead to me having to tell my daddy that I lost my virginity. Yes, I had that talk with my father and his response was, "Tootie, you know daddy will always love you, but I'm telling you to leave that nappy-headed little boy alone. If I catch you around him, I will flash."

Dee and I had to sneak to see each other and pass notes through his cousin at school. One day he kept walking in front Bob and his girlfriend, Erykah, house. My mom and Erykah saw the hurt in my eyes as I watched him, so they offered to let Dee come in and sit with me. Not telling my uncle, that they allowed him to come there made a happy situation turn into a brutal one. Bob was under the impression that I snuck the little boy in my little cousin, Moon didn't make it any better. She was mad because we kicked her out of the room. Moon was the cousin that was always snitching and stealing, so we always knew to leave her in the dark. She went run lie to Bob about us doing the nasty in the room because she was mad at us.

Dee had a Bebe gun we were playing with, and I accidentally shot Michelle with it. Before she could even make it out the room to tell. Boom! There goes my uncle bursting into the room. "Bob" is what I called him because he reminded me so much of Bob from La Bamba. He told Dee he had to leave because, like the hot boy he was, he was all over me. Bob then called my mom and me in the bathroom, I was thinking he was about to whip me with a belt. Oh, baby did we think wrong. Bob was so drunk that I pushed him down and took his belt from him. While my momma screamed, "Bob get your ass up before she hit you with your own belt."

I politely left out of the bathroom, got on the phone, and called my daddy. My daddy had a rule— no one except my mom could lay a finger on me. Within five minutes of me calling my daddy, he busted through the door ready to jump on Bob. My momma being the narcissist she was, lied and acted like it was all my fault. I was used to it by that age. I didn't have a care in the world about what they had to say because they allowed their friend, a man I called and treated like my uncle, to do inappropriate things with me and get away with it. Covering the whole incident up. If only I would have known that holding a grudge against them wasn't hurting them but was instead hurting me.

Once my daddy heard that Dee was there, he went crazy! He grabbed me by the neck and pinned me up against the wall. He screamed in my face, "You're still messing with him after I told you to leave him alone?"

What really took the cake was when he told me to pack my stuff because I was going to stay with Dee. He told me, "Let's see if that little nigga is going to take care of you."

My father never laid a finger on me before, so it really hurt my heart more than it hurt my face when he slapped me.

Once outside, I noticed the whole block was full of people. The Oil Mill was always off the chain every day, 24/7, 365 daily back then. It wasn't until I noticed that Dee was walking up the street with my godbrother, Shakeith, that I knew it was about to go down. My daddy went up to Dee and slapped the spit out of his mouth, leaving his pretty yellow face with a handprint. Everybody came running screaming, "No, Bird, let the little boy make it don't do that."

Even Ms. Emma came running and saying, "No, Bird, her momma let him go in there.

Bird please."

When I saw my daddy slap him, I took off running to my friend, Sha, house. Five minutes later, I hear a knock on her door. I tried to tell her not to answer it, but she did anyway and there my daddy stood. "Sha, where Kay at?"

Sha saw the look on my daddy's face and got scared, so she gave me up. Once I stepped on the porch, the slapping began again. My daddy really thought Dee and I did something that night, but we didn't. Once again, I was slapped walking down the road until we got in front of where Ms. Emma was, and finally, she got through to him about what really happened.

Meanwhile, the cops were pulling up. My daddy hurried and called my momma from in the house while he tried to prepare his story in his head that he didn't hit the boy. Even the cops saw the handprint in Dee face, but in their head, they were thinking hell I would have done the same thing for my daughter, so he let my daddy go.

While the cops were leaving, my grandmother was pulling up on her bike. She was tickled pink by the fact that the little boy was only eleven and I was fourteen. Y'all need to be happy they didn't take your daughter to jail for robbing the cradle. My Momo Wanda had no filter and said whatever came to mind. She was very bold with it too, sometimes even aggressive. Come to find out she had found out through Dee's daddy, Lee, that he was lying about his age the whole time. It was almost a year that we had been fooling around and I didn't know this.

That beating my daddy gave me set me straight

because I ended up staying away from Dee and right before my eyes, he did exactly what my father said he would do—. Mess with one of the girls that I was hanging with and spread around the town that he slept with me. At that point, I knew exactly why my daddy used to sing "S.E.X" by Lyfe Jennings to me. My daddy loved music, he was a rapper and was very good at it too. He was really respected and known not to be messed with, and because of that, I had the same respect in return. My daddy made me move back in with him to make sure I never stepped foot close to Dee again. Of course, we sent letters through his cousin that went to my school because she stayed with him, but things weren't the same.

My momma ended up meeting this guy named "Q." He was one of my uncles' old friends that use to hang out by my grandmother's house in Brick Yard. She had moved in with him and brought my siblings with her as well. This is the man that gave her a black eye because she had my daddy in his house when he got off from work. He and my daddy passed words because my momma made a remark about Q whipping me and that's all my daddy had to hear before he blew up. "Ain't no nigga whipping my daughter, are you crazy?"

Next thing you know, Q said that he wasn't going to whip anyone else's kids because that wasn't his place. But he and my daddy still almost got into a fistfight. That ended with my daddy speeding off in his truck on two wheels. Sweet Pea and I just sat there listening to him go off about going get his gun, but I told my grandmother on my daddy before he could even hit the door to leave out the house. The next day, my daddy and I were walking when he told me about Q giving my momma a black eye because of what went down at his house. He said that he was going to kill that nigga.

As we were walking, we ran into Moe and Dee, my daddy said to pay close attention to Dee and my so-called friend. "They hand playing too much", he said, as me and him walked to the corner store called Popillion. I asked him sarcastically, "I thought you said I couldn't even look his way daddy?"

But I did, and I saw what he saw. I just brushed it off saying, "Daddy they're friends too."

But before you know it, the hood was telling me that they were messing around. To be honest, I didn't even care. So, when I went by Sha's house after school, he snuck to see me, and I didn't have too many words for him this time. I remember Latifah saying, "Baby, you will have many loves in your lifetime."

And now I know why.

The school year had ended and all Summer long I was under my daddy's supervision, literally his shadow. Everywhere he was at, I was there too. We would talk about everything from the streets to how much important it was to never let anyone see you sweat. Only the strong survive.

Chapter Three
Dreaming-Young Jezzy

That Summer, I started having weird dreams. I kept seeing Yvette crying at a crime scene with cops blocking both ends of our street off. I couldn't see what for, but my spirit was telling me it was about my father. Especially after his wife, Nikki, cut his arm open with a glass bottle. The meat under his skin and bones were showing. I kept telling my grandmother, "Wait until I get older, I'm going to show her."

But Yvette had then beat the crap out of her. How could my daddy be so smart but get caught up with a woman like that? As we sat watching his favorite movie, "Shottas," Diamond, our family pit bull, was steady licking my daddy's scar. My grandmother said she was licking it to heal it faster. That night, I told my daddy I was having weird dreams that I knew were about him and that he needed to be careful. He turned and said, "Tootie, I'm going to get us out of the hood and in a nice house just for us.

Every footstep he made, I was right behind him, because my gut was telling me don't leave his side. Even though he was absent for a long time throughout my life, my daddy was all I really had. He made me feel so special and I knew I was always safe with him. Hell, he made it clear he would lay someone down for playing with me.

One late night we sat on Yvette's porch until 2 or 3 o'clock in the morning. Even though he hustled for a living, he never let me witness him doing it. See my daddy and his crew was in the streets because they had to be. That's the only thing they knew that could triple their income and feed their family. My daddy had it hard. Momo Wanda was smoking the very same thing he was selling. But back then they had codes and boundaries for what you couldn't do when hustling. The No.1 rule was to take care of the kids and elderly. Protect and keep them safe. Our street soldiers are what they were. My daddy wouldn't dare sell a crumb to my grandmother and would blow her high every time she was in the bathroom. He would go scream, "Wanda!"

"Get the fuck away from the door, Courtney!" my grandmother would say, calling him by his government name.

My father got tired of beating up and confronting others for selling drugs to my grandmother, so he finally accepted it. But tried his best to blow her high every time. Growing up, he watched his mother go through a very hard time. He promised her that once he got old enough and big enough, he would never allow anyone to hurt her again. My Momo Wanda told me stories about how when they were homeless, my father used to watch over her as they slept under trees. Also, that they would take turns looking after one another every night. I could tell that the past still hurt her because you could hear the hurt in her voice when she would tell the story. She did the best that she knew how to take care of her kids, no she wasn't the mother of the year, but she tried. "If I could go back in time, Tootie, I would change it all around," she would tell me when the pain of not giving life her best sunk in.

She tried to make up for that with Sweet Pea and me with movie nights, bike rides, walks, and midnight snacks. She couldn't do any wrong in our eyes, even when she would flash out and beat us up, we still loved her.

After Nikki cut my daddy's arm open, he finally cut ties and I loved it. In fact, I loved it so much I wouldn't talk about any of his new friends to their faces anymore. I rather see him with them than her. But I did have some words about them. From this light-skin chick, BeeBop sister, and Ronnie... I didn't care. I was very territorial and jealous about my daddy and all of the women he came across knew it because I let it be known. "Tootie you don't care what comes out your mouth," he would say.

So, he got to the point where he wouldn't bring his flings to meet me anymore. My daddy was a daddy to Yvette and D'wana as well because their daddy walked out on them a while ago. That Summer, I hit my first blunt with Loe and Dashiki, Ronnie's sisters right behind our house on the train track. I didn't even know how to inhale it, but I wanted to smoke. Loe and Dashiki weren't new to it, so they knew how to roll and inhale it. That was a story I kept from my daddy because of all of the contact highs I caught from being around him, I may as well hit it.

At that time, Loe liked me, hell probably even loved me but for some reason, I just didn't look at him like that. Yvette was dating his older brother BeeBop and D'wana was starting something up with the middle brother, Jay. I didn't want any part of that circle and their momma, Ms. Shake, was just like my Momo Wanda and equally crazy as well. The two in the same room were a big hot mess. They would argue until they couldn't holler anymore. Everyone that was around would always move away because of the hollering match between them two. Therefore, I had enough craziness with my grandmother to have a mother-in-law just as crazy. Loe knew my daddy would approve, so he tried, but I kept turning him down. My daddy even asked why I didn't like him, I just simply kept saying, "I don't know, I just don't."

That Summer, I had my eyes on B, but he was much older than me and I knew my daddy would kill him so I would just watch him. His daughter, Kyle, and I were best friends' way before he got out of prison. I don't know if it was his tattoos or his body frame, but whichever one it was, it had my nose wide open. He knew it too. I would catch him looking every now and then, but he knew no matter what he couldn't touch me or that would be his funeral. So, we just watched one another, never once touching or even a wink of an eye.

My daddy made it clear that year that he knew a few of his associates were watching me. While on Yvette's porch, he said, "The main ones laughing and smiling in my face be the same ones watching my daughter."

I didn't understand what he was saying because in my head I was thinking, Dang daddy, nobody wants to mess with me because of you. Being green to the fact that just because they were scared doesn't mean that they weren't thinking about it. Not knowing I was in for a rude awakening. The dreams about something happening to my daddy kept coming through. I tried to warn him by telling him and sticking really close to him because even though we had our disagreements I love my daddy to death. I couldn't protect him the way I wanted to though. My mother and my nanny Mariah ended up stopping by our house to get some issue from my daddy. Next thing you know, my momma is asking him if I could come to help her with my siblings for a little while, and even though I said no, my daddy still told me to go.

Did he not understand what I told him? Why was he pushing me off now? When just last night I had him listen to "26 years and 17 days" by Lyfe Jennings that brought tears to his eyes. I was warning him that it was time to change before life changes for him, but I still just packed a few things and went with them.

Chapter Four
26 years 17 days-Lyfe Jennings

Almost two weeks passed by after I had left from my daddy. My cousins— Michelle, Moon, and Poppa—made me forget all about worrying about my father because we were having so much fun. We were doing all kinds of things: swimming, going all down the gully and getting into all kinds of stuff. But I was in for a rude awakening. A few mornings later at around 6 o'clock, my Nanny Mariah was banging on the FEMA trailer we moved in with this guy named, Bernard, that my momma met that worked offshore. He was never home so my mother, siblings, and I stayed there when he was at work. When they woke me up, I knew something wasn't right, all I can remember is my Nanny Mariah saying, "Hurry, brush your teeth and get dressed something happened to Bird. My whole body went numb, even though my feet were hitting the ground, I couldn't feel anything. My mind went blank, and all of my body just felt out of whack. Like my soul was leaving me.

I could hear them talking but I couldn't register any of it. My body was with them, but baby my spirit was with my father. The whole ride there I kept repeating, practically screaming, in my head, You must be okay, daddy, you can't just leave me like that! You can't just leave me all alone, please!

In the midst of that, I heard my Nanny Mariah say, "Vera, the girl is going to lose it, you know how close her, and Bird is."

Once we made it to the Oil Mill from Carencro, I immediately saw the block was full and any time the whole hood is out at that time in the morning meant that something had happened. I saw my Momo Wanda pacing the sidewalk, when she saw me get out of the car, she ran to me. "Tootie, they shot him... they shot Bird."

I felt everyone's eyes on me as I maneuvered to Yvette. She was telling the crowd what happened and that if my daddy wouldn't have been on the porch, the dude would have shot up her house.

The story was that this dude named Rodney from California came up to Yvette project on a bike looking for BeeBop. My daddy asked him what he wanted because BeeBop was in the house for the night. He told my daddy he wanted him to trade some rocks for weed. My daddy then told him he would buy the rocks from him so he could buy him some weed. But once he gave the rocks to my daddy, he immediately put it in his mouth to see if it was real. When my daddy noticed it was fake, he started punching him down and his whole crew (Adrian, Scoey, Pep, Travis, and Big Dee) joined in. But if the guy would have done his homework, he would have known not to even play with my daddy like that. He also should have known that if anyone saw my daddy fighting in the hood, they were jumping in rather he was winning or not. My daddy had a rep for taking care of his loved ones and was very loyal when it came down to the dos and don'ts; he paid his dues and he been earned his respect.

As they were beating him, he took off running and banging on the neighbor's door for someone to help him. He was so mad and ashamed about what happened until it made him have murder on his mind. Later that night he came back sneaking up from the cut behind the house only to find my father on the porch by himself. He started shooting, meanwhile, bullets were bouncing off of the wall. His crew had then gone their separate ways leaving only my daddy outside. Adrian didn't even make it through the door good before he heard the shots fired. The fool could have shot his self the way the bullets were bouncing off of the wall. Even though my daddy had a chance to brace himself, his arm couldn't shield him from the hot bullets that hit his arm, head, and lower body. When Adrian ran outside to see what was going on, he found my daddy slumped over on the porch. My Momo Wanda came out screaming and hollering, "No Bird!"

The only reason why the guy got caught is because he came back to get revenge on my daddy's crew at the scene. As soon as Rodney touched the parish, my daddy's best friend, Big Dee, broke his jaw. He got jumped a couple of times, they had to ship him off. The guards even knew that my daddy had a rep, and the guys weren't going to stop until they killed him. We found out that the dude was down here because he killed someone in California and was here hiding out. My father not only got caught slipping that night but had given his gun to Fat Rat so he couldn't get back at him if he had the chance to.

They waited for me to load up and leave. Once we got to the hospital, the doctor immediately came out and told us that my father might not make it and if he did, he would be a "vegetable". I knew my daddy wouldn't just leave me like that, he couldn't... he promised me he would never leave me again. But there he was laying in the hospital bed with his head wrapped and bandages all over his body. This can't be real life, I kept thinking. I also thought of all the things that I had been through and now this. I barely had time with my father, and now this man just tries to take him from me. I didn't understand how pride could cause a man to react this way. His ego was crushed and that was the only method he could think of to fix it. Then for him to walk through the trail behind Yvette's house and sneak up on my father and not give him a chance to defend himself was a coward move. He could have come back and fought him one on one, my daddy would have fought him fair and square. He didn't tell his click to jump in, they did that themselves.

Why my father lord? My father must have felt the worry and how afraid I was feeling because I knew my life would never be the same from that point on. Through all the surgeries, needles, and testes my father pushed through. The doctor let us know they would have to ship my father to Plaquemine. Him not having health insurance played a big role in his care. Yvette had to apply for him to get Medicaid just to get the service he needed.

My father was now two hours from home and the only one that had a car was Yvette's boyfriend, BeeBop, and let's just say these rides were interesting. Once we made it to see my father, we notice that he couldn't talk, walk, or use the bathroom on his own but he knew who we were. When he saw us walk into the room his eyes lit up with excitement and love. He even winked his eye at me letting me know he knew who I was. Despite the doctors saying he wouldn't remember a thing he did. I sat at the edge of his bed just looking at him. He was holding on like the soldier he was.

At that point, he had gotten skinny because he was getting fed through a tube in his stomach. I didn't like the sight of it, but I held my composer. I couldn't let him see worry or scaredness of any kind. We wanted him to believe that he was going to make it out just fine. When it was time to leave that night, that's when reality sunk in that he wasn't coming home with us and not only did it hurt but a part of me stayed with him. On the way to get on the highway, the cops pulled us over because (1) we were in an old school roadmaster with tinted windows and (2) had a deep aroma of weed. BeeBop didn't have a license, but Meg did and that's why they put her in the car with us, just in case we got pulled over. Meg wasn't the right candidate at the time because someone had slipped her some type of drug and the once pretty young lady was now lost in the streets. The cops weren't aware of this though, so they let us go with a warning. Once Meg got behind the wheel, everyone was hollering, "Oh no! Pullover at the first store you see."

Lord, our lives were in danger in the blink of an eye, literally. Once she pulled over, BeeBop took the wheel, and we were home in no time.

Since my daddy was in the condition, he was in, Yvette stood up to raise me. Even though I was practically raising myself by then. I heard so many times to get it how you live until I thought that this was the only way. Yeah, she did what she could, but it wasn't genuine like my father. In my family, instead of the older women being positive role models, they were examples of what not to be. Their lives evolved around mean so much that they couldn't keep the focus of the matters at hand because they were chasing behind them all day and night.

Chapter Five
Coming from where I'm from-Anthony Hamilton

Before my father was shot, my little cousin Sweet Pea's foot was run over by a train due to him playing on the moving train that passed behind our project in the Mill. It was right around the time I was holding a grudge against my father for beating me because of Dee. They tried to revive it, but they couldn't, and my little cousin now had to be in a wheelchair because his foot was cut off to save the rest of his leg.

Yvette was working two jobs at that time. So, we didn't have a bedtime and went to sleep whenever we wanted to. We watched whatever we wanted to and seen all kinds of drug transactions daily at the house. It got to the point where one day I had to act like I needed something when the cops raided the house, just to get some dope out of the house through the back door to Co. The police still found what they came for, but it wasn't all of it. Yvette took the charge and went to jail because it was her house. Not only did she go to jail, but she lost her project and we had to move immediately. That happened just a week before we got in a wreck going see my daddy because BeeBop ran straight into the back of an eighteen-wheeler while Yvette and I were asleep in the back. We didn't even make it to my daddy that day. BeeBop not only didn't have his license but didn't have insurance either, so he had to do a U-turn through the grass in the middle of the highway to get on the opposite side of the highway to head home before he went to jail.

That white girl has a way of sneaking up on you. Even though Cody came to be the designated driver with a license, we still ended up in a tough situation. I realized that I never had a childhood, I had to grow up well before my time.

The whole way home, Yvette was fussing and cursing, meanwhile, I noticed when I hit the back of BeeBop's seat so hard that I bit a chunk out of the inside of my lip. How we made it back with the whole hood pushed in and radiator busted was a miracle, everyone said.

Yvette ended up taking church more seriously saying that she was going to quit smoking weed, cursing, and fighting. My father told her before he got shot that he would come with us to church one day, he told her to wait for him. Did he feel death around the corner?

My daddy bounced around from hospital to hospital until finally, Yvette got him placed closer to home in a hospital in Eunice. Yvette and BeeBop ended up moving by Opelousas Junior High School, down the gravel road in the very last trailer. At this point, I was in the Eight grade with a whole lot of self-confidence and boldness, but I still hung out with the guys. Hell, the whole time I was at OJ, I got in trouble because I was always around when something took place but wouldn't say anything. When Pumpa or Rakius wasn't getting me in trouble that year was the question? If I could only go back to those days.

That year, I ended up leaving Yvette's house because I felt like she was being too strict, and I wasn't comfortable there anymore like I used to be when my daddy was staying there. Things just weren't the same anymore. I moved back in with my Momo Cindy in her one-bedroom apartment that I had to share space and room with my Uncle Snoop, Bob, Papa GA, Uncle Chuck, Latifa, Moon, my three siblings, Michelle, and Poppa. All of us living together in that little space was not easy, but we made it happen. I ended up having to go to Beau Chene.

Being back around my family made me happy and gave me life again. I was starting to feel happy again. I tried not to worry too much about my daddy, so I stayed busy. My momma ended up telling me that she was moving to Lake Charles and asked if I could go with her to help with the kids. I didn't want to go at all because she was going out there to live in a shelter. It's not like we hadn't before, we stayed in a shelter when I was in the sixth grade before she went to St. Gabriel for writing bad checks. I hid my fears well then, but this was different. We would be moving somewhere I didn't know anyone. Even though my Momo Cindy was originally from there, all we ever knew was Opelousas because my grandmother was given up for adoption and ended up there. I was originally born in Lake Charles.

It was hard for me to just leave the life I always knew behind. But being the soft-hearted person I was, I fell for it and went with her. We stayed with over twenty different women and their kids. The only good thing was that we had our own beds to sleep in. I kept up with my friends from Opelousas on My Space, a very popular website at the time that enabled you to send messages and view other's pages. Facebook was around at the time, but I heard it was mainly for college students. We had family there too, but it didn't feel like back home. My baby sister, Athena, wasn't having it at all. She cried day in and day out. My momma ended up registering me at S.J. Welsh high school for the rest of the year. Three different schools in one year, but this school wasn't like back home at all. For the first time ever, I was seeing girls my age dating other girls all through the hallways like that was cool. Things were totally different, I felt it. My momma had to end up sending Athena back home because she literally cried all day long and my momma couldn't take it because she had bad nerves. My little brother was like five kids in one, giving her all kinds of trouble with his bad temper. He would ram his head on the ground every time things didn't go the way he wanted them to.

After three months of living in the women's shelter, my mom ended up moving into one of their houses across the street. It was a two-bedroom with three beds. It wasn't all that, but it was a place to call our home. Our family from back home even started visiting and having all kinds of get together, we were always having fun. One day when we all gathered by Pandora's house is when things started to change. My Nanny, Mariah, fell into seizer right in the driveway of Pandora's house and hit her head then caught another one at my momma's house. It was so bad that she peed on herself. I was crying like hell; I was always soft-hearted, just hide it really well. As my momma did her best for her to come out of the seizer, I called 911. My momma kept praying to God that she pulls through. It's like there's always a warning before destruction came into my family.

The next morning, before my grandmother left, she told me that my momma had gotten some income tax money for me and not my brother that she lied to me. Which caused me to miss prom. I didn't have a dress, nor my hair done. Lake Charles school was like back home in a way there were always the popular kids and the kids that didn't have much. Why was society created like this? I always wondered since they printed money, then why wouldn't they give enough of it to all of us. As I kissed my grandmother goodbye, I knew then I was ready to go back home. My grandmother never ever lied to me; she always told the truth. But as for me, growing up I lied about having things I didn't have so no one would know how less fortunate I was. One of the girls at S.J. knew though, so she would give me all of her old name brand clothes she didn't want. Her mother and daddy were business owners and well off. My momma thought I was stealing out of the mall, and I let her think exactly what she wanted to because it didn't matter what I said anyway.

To make matters even worse, we ended up getting into a fight due to her drinking and mixing it with drugs. This was nothing new she always beat on me or take her frustration out on me. Clauddine, my grandmother's sister, was there to stop it and told me to just take a walk. As I walked off, I called my grandmother on my Tracfone which was called a biscuit crying telling her what just happened. Next thing you know, the guy, Matt, that lived next door to us that I had a crush on was outside and saw me crying and came running after me down the street saying I could come to his house. Once I was inside, there were boys everywhere; he said his momma had five boys and one girl. He led me to his room, turned his TV on, told me to get comfortable, and then left out of the room. He had to tell his momma four times that he knew I was younger than him because she kept expressing that, she didn't want him to get in trouble. When he came back in the room, he promised that he wouldn't get me in any trouble. He explained that he saw my momma and me having an altercation while he was going to the washhouse behind his house. He said it would probably be safer for me to spend the night there. Telling me his mother agreed as well.

She was only being a concerned mother. I told him I totally understood where she was coming from. He just said that she was tripping. The only thing on my mind was to get back home to my grandmother. It was time for me to go. How did it look for me to be sleeping at a guy's house that I didn't even know? He gave me one of his big T-shirts and promised he wouldn't let anything happen to me. It didn't even take me thirty minutes to fall asleep.

When I woke up the room was still pitch black from the foil paper on his bedroom window. I heard guys talking outside and he wasn't in the bed, so I knew he was out there too. I put my clothes on and went towards the door. Once I opened it, the sun had blinded me. When he saw me, he smiled a warm smile asking if I slept well. His brothers were looking puzzled because they didn't know I was in the house and of course the first thing that came to their minds was that we had done something together. He told them to stop being jackasses and then he walked me to where our yard ends and his yard began. He gave me his number and told me to call him any time. When I walked into our house, my Auntie Clauddine was sitting on the sofa and my momma was still sleeping in the bed. Where were you girl? I was so worried about you. I told your momma she was wrong for that. Come here let me see your face. "Oh, hell no!" she screamed.

"Go get that cocoa butter so I can put it on you."

Once in the bathroom, I glance at my face for the first time. She had scratched the skin off of my face and I now had a scar-like Scar from the movie "The Lion

King". The first thought that came to my mind when I saw my face in the mirror was that the guy Matt had saw it too, and it made me feel instantly embarrassed. As I walked with my head down to my Auntie Clauddine, she lifted my head in her hand and applied the cocoa butter to my cut and told me to put it on it every day so that the scar can go away. I stayed in my room that whole night listening to my CD player, hoping and wishing someone would just take me away from here. Next door, Matt and his brothers were having a party and they had the music blasting, so I didn't call him that night. I was more focused on getting away from here. I didn't want to go to school or anywhere anymore with that big scratch on my face. But I was forced to and ended up getting in a fight at my drop-off with a girl named Aweava. I took my frustration out on her and whooped her ass.

As I walked away from the fight, breathing hard, I saw Matt and his brother sitting on the porch they were watching the whole time. He came to the end of the street asking me why I never called. The truth is I was shame and he sensed it. He smiled those pearly white teeth at me and told me to call him. Meanwhile, his brother was laughing saying, "Damn, you beat the crap out of that girl. What did she do to you man?"

Matt gave him a look to be quiet. I told him that I would call him later and he asked, "You sure?"

"Yes, I'm sure," I responded.

What did he want from me, I wondered as I walked home.

I was an 8th grader, and he wasn't even in school anymore. But me being me, I still called him.

He wanted me to come over that night, asking if my momma would let me, and I told him she doesn't care. My Uncle Chuck had moved in with us around that time, but he would only be there to watch us when my momma was at work. She was working at Ashley Furniture Store at the time. I put some clothes on and went to meet him next door. Everybody there was way older than me. I was very nervous to be around him, but he told me it was okay and to just chill.

We sat next to each other on the porch while everyone else was laughing and joking. Then, all of a sudden, he offered for me to come inside his house. Soon as I walked in his house, he started kissing me everywhere, from my lips to my forehead, to my neck. What is he doing? I asked myself. I tried to back away, but he insisted that I let him make me feel better. I finally backed away and told him that I was scared. At that point, it had been almost two years since I lost my virginity to Dee. Plus, I'd never had sex with anyone older than me. Then he said, "I'm going to go slow."

I let him grab my hand and guide me into his room. He then laid me onto his bed and did something with his tongue I had never felt before, then put himself inside of me. Which wasn't easy and hurt like hell, but I just laid there and let him have his way. "I'm going to be gentle," he kept whispering in my ear.

How did we end up here, I kept wondering in my head. It felt like he was taking my soul with every stroke. An hour later, there I was laying numb while he wiped me and told me he never had something like "that" before. He acted gentle and loving, holding and caressing my body like I'd never felt before. As he walked me out, I told him that I was going home because my stomach was hurting but the truth is everything was hurting, and he knew by the way I was walking, and of course his brothers noticed too. "That's what y'all was doing?" they asked while laughing and the girls they were with were laughing as well.

Personally, I didn't see anything funny, I was in

pain. Matt stood up for me and told them to stop being childish, but one brother still went as far as asking "How was it?" and slapping his arm.

He told them to hush and told me not to worry about them, and to go home and take a bath, everything should be okay. He lied! When I peed, it burnt like razor blades. My little "sally bowl" was even ripped and bleeding a little bit. After I got out of the tub, I jumped into my bed and went straight to sleep.

The next day, I went to school and told Brucy about my night and asked her if it was normal for it to burn and hurt when I pee. She said, "Yeah girl, it's been a long time for you.

"You were practically a virgin again."

She coached me about a lot of girl things because I didn't know as much as she did. So, I always listened to the stories she told about her boy experiences. After school that day, I saw Matt's oldest brother outside sitting in his car, so I went to holler at him before I went into the house. Matt's oldest brother and I had been cool way before he and I. We would hang almost every day outside and I even introduced him to Ternika, my new friend I met at school. The time would fly by when we would chill. One day, my little brother, Duttie, got a hold of his male enhancement pills and ate two then was on my Aunt Tiwona's car doing the Michael Jackson sound "ew ew." We nearly died from laughing! Meanwhile, I clowned him by asking, "Why do you even have that stuff."

He laughed saying, "Hey! A man must be a man."

When we would hang, I used to hardly see Matt around because he was always on the go, but his brother caught my undivided attention when he made a joke about us having sex in return. He didn't know it, but it hurt my feelings. Matt said he wouldn't tell anyone but yet he did. How could I be so stupid? No wonder why all of sudden his momma didn't want me in her yard. She thought I was fast, but Matt's big brother didn't care, he still let me come over all of the time. They momma was tripping because she found some nasty texts on her phone from Matt and I. Brucy is who really told me what to text Matt while we were at school coaching me on what to say. Hell, I didn't know any better, I was five years younger than him. I stayed my distance after what his oldest brother told me because my feelings were hurt, and my pride was scarred. That's why when my momma said she found us a new house I wasn't sad or mad about the move.

The shelter gave my momma a month to find another house because she was having too many guests and they were monitoring her every move. My momma hated that. Even though we moved, I still went to S.J. Welsh, I just rode a different bus and was living in an actual house then. The only thing that sucked was at the old house we had hot water, but momma couldn't afford it at the new house. So, we had to warm our water up in the microwave to take a bath. At the old house, the shelter paid all of the bills and furnished the house… we just lived there. My Uncle Chuck made it fun though. He even let me smoke weed for the weed with him and told me not to start tripping because he was going to act like nothing ever happened.

My momma found a Mexican boyfriend that was living across the street from our Auntie Betty at the time. He was weird; he would watch me all of the time until one day my momma asked him if he liked me. He just grinned and shook his head no. He ended up getting ran off by my momma's other friend, PeeWee, who drug him out of the bed while My Uncle Chuck, my siblings, and I were laying down in the front room. My Uncle Chuck missed everything because he took a Seroquel and was knocked out. Bob, who came to town that night too, started talking shit to PeeWee because he drugged the Mexican out of the bed. You see, Bob thought he was Mexican and always spoke a foreign language that was neither Spanish nor anything else we understood. He told PeWee to step outside with his Penguin, SpongeBob-looking ass. Not knowing he had his ten-foot big quarter-back cousin in our room laying down. When PeeWee knocked on our room door to call his cousin out of the room, it was then that my Uncle Bob knew he couldn't stand a chance.

The only thing he could think of was to slap Uncle Chuck on his legs to try and wake him up. Saying, "Chuck, get up get up they have a big mother f***** in here."

Uncle Chuck didn't bulge. He was out from the pill he took earlier. Once Bob noticed he was alone in this fight he immediately rethought the whole thing and started partying with them instead. Once I saw everything was fine, I laid my head down and continued watching tv in the front room until the tv watched me.

I guess me switching three different schools in one year had its toll on my grades because I received a letter in the mail saying I had to repeat the eighth grade. My momma didn't trip or say anything about me failing as a normal parent would. I been grown in her eyes. She hadn't had to wake me up or tell me to get ready for school since I was in the fourth grade. I pretty much taught myself how to be responsible in that.

Chapter Six
Misunderstood- Lil Wayne

So, there I was catching the bus faithfully every day. One day, I got off of the bus and my momma was telling me that Clauddine would be staying with us for a while. I started spending every night at my new friend's house I met at Summer school name Marshayla. At her house, she had a computer, hot water, and siblings her age. My momma didn't even ask to meet her parents like my grandmother used to. Momo Cindy did not let me go spend the night anywhere. She was very overprotective. I only went home when I missed my brother and sister or to hang with Uncle Chuck. At that point, it did not surprise me when my Cousin Cool J pulled up with the woman that was dating the man that Clauddine was in the room with at our house. If anything, it was funny as hell and my momma kept yelling, "Kay, shut the hell up. Nothing is funny!"

But I could not stop laughing at Cool J saying, "But momma, that is this woman's man. He took her check, and now he's over here with you," he explained.

Clauddine yelled, "Cool J, you messy bitch! Do you see what he did Vera? He let that woman take my man."

At that point, I was rolling on the floor in tears laughing, while my momma slapped me, telling me to shut up. Even when it was over, I kept bursting out laughing. Cool J was not making it any better when he said, "Vera, I am hungry."

Then Clauddine screamed, "So what bastard, starve!"

I nearly died from laughter. Even my momma was laughing, telling Cool J to go ahead and fix a sandwich in the kitchen. After a while of them going back and forth, he said,

"Fine! You do not want me here, I am going. But that's still that woman's man."

"You son of bitch!" she screamed, as he walked out of the house laughing.

After a few hours, she went on about it until she got over it and opened a beer. When everything and everyone was quiet, and I was alone, I wondered and even prayed for a better life than this. It was not fair. Why me? I questioned. Shouldn't little girls be blessed with the world and a stable home? Silly me, I always thought maybe if I found love through a boy, I would be that girl I always saw in other girls.

So, it didn't take much for Devontea to slide his slick self in. By me making the first move writing him a note saying I liked him, we went on from there. We talked on the phone all day and night. I wrote his name on damn near everything that belonged to me. He would write me little poems and slide them to me. However, I found out he was my little cousin Waylo's cousin on his momma's daddy side of the family.

We were inseparable living our best of life until someone from summer school told the other girl that, he was dating as well on the low that he would be hugged up with me after school. So, when she popped up at school, he went straight for the bus. He couldn't even look me in the eye before leaving on the bus that afternoon. That evening, I called his grandmother's house as soon as I got home, but he was not there. Was that it because I could not move around how he did. The whole time we were talking, we never got as far as seeing one another naked.

That night, I went to sleep confused and hurt. The next day at school, it showed; I just lounged around until he came and pulled me to the side saying he was sorry and that I was his girl. He even made me his second friend on his MySpace page. Talking about making a girl feel special. We never had a chance to see each other outside of school, so we talked on the phone for hours instead. Of course, when he was in the house because he ran the streets a lot. He had tattoos in the eighth grade, which was something I never saw back home. I strongly believed that is what made me attracted to him. Unaware that I was attracted to boys from around the way and looked at the nice, sweet boys as squares. If only then I knew I was going to be taking on a roller coaster ride by those types of guys. After a month of letters and poems, holding hands, and kissing, I received a letter saying he did not want to be my boyfriend anymore.

That jive-talking, charming, brown-skinned, pretty smile, and relaxing vibe type of guy was now knocking the very breath he made me breathe right out of me. Then, there in the middle of the hall was me in tears sobbing out of control. What in the hell had he just done to me? I questioned. What did I do? Was it because I could not be with him outside of school because he stayed on the other end of Lake Charles?

Even though Marshayla and her cousin, Zana, were trying to comfort me by taking me into the girl's bathroom and telling me he was an asshole, I did not want to hear it. They did not understand that he made me feel a feeling I never felt before. Like I was beautiful and worthy.

I didn't grow up with a momma nor father around 24/7 to make me know and feel like that. I felt stupid and hurt especially when my ex, Mark, witnessed it. Damn, now two boys had broken up with me. This explains exactly why I let the guy, Matt, from next door score on the second day of being around him. Now, I really was confused when you don't or can't have sex with boys, they break up with you... and even when you do, they don't speak to you the next day. What do they want then?

Zana explained that she didn't have sex with her boyfriend until they were together for 8 months and they still were together. I didn't say it out loud but, in my head, I was saying, Yeah, that's because you're pretty, high class, with good hair, and a mother that dresses you up in Hollister. While I am black with, not short, but not too long hair, clothes that came from the shelter, and only name brand shoes I get is during income tax time. Zana had guys dying to be with her, while boys use to hide that, they liked me back home. What a life to live?

Then the Leap test was going on and I couldn't even focus. The only thing that was on my mind was getting away from Lake Charles. I was then missing back home.

As soon as the Leap testing was over, we went to visit Opelousas just to witness Hurricane Katrina take place. I was so happy to see Kyle; I thought I would never see her again. During Katrina, we stayed up until 6 o'clock in the morning eating thirty dollars' worth of candy that Big Two let us spend off my momma food stamp card. After she told us to only spend ten dollars before we left with him to go to the store. We talked for hours about my life in Lake Charles and her life down here in Opelousas.

Kyle and I were like Vanilla and Chocolate. We did everything together and told one another everything. You'd swear we were born together. We even dated two brothers once, Casey and D-Low. Like any normal female best friends, we had our fights over the phone, talked about what to watch next, and who was tougher than the other. But we stuck together like glue and were on go for each other. I was a little older than her, so I was always willing to take up for her. So, naturally, she was the first to know that I had a crush on her daddy and had been knowing since before I left for Lake Charles. She just kept saying, "Guh, that is on y'all."

Kyle never judged me once. She knew that I took a liking to her father because she knew my story. Plus, around that age, most of the girls I knew and came up with were dating older men. That is why they would sit alone or be flirting with dudes on campus but never saw them hugging or kissing them. I knew I wanted him and was not stopping until I had him.

Once I get something in my head, I do not stop until I get it, good or bad for me. Hell, somebody could tell me the stove was hot and I would still try to touch it just to see if it would burn me. At that age, I was like a lion choosing its prey. I studied B for years. First, it started with eye contact, then, I would brush up on him to see how he would react. That Summer, I sensed that I could go in with my move. After the third night in the bad storm, I ended up sneaking into B's bed and sharing my body with him. It had been over 6 months since I last had sex, so it hurt but also felt good. I guess because I had been wanting to be with him in that way, my body reacted in a way that, I never saw it act before. There I was on top of a 28-year-old man, and I just knew what to do. It was like my body had a mind of its own. "God damn, Kay!" was all I heard.

As we went up and down, he whispered my name telling me he was going to take care of me. "You're for me," he told me as he held my head kissing me all over my face and body.

After we were done, he told me, "Now I do not want you to share that with nobody else," pointing at my private area.

He knew he did not have to tell me not to say anything because he knew I wouldn't. Somehow, he knew I knew not to talk my business.

Chapter Seven
Let Me Love You Down-
Ready for the World

I didn't go back with my momma to Lake Charles after the storm. Instead, I told her I was going to stay with Yvette that school year instead. I knew if I stayed in Opelousas B, and I would be able to sneak off from time to time. Every field trip to the mall B snuck and sent me money through Kyle. Yvette questioned where I was getting all that stuff from, I came up with a lie that my friend Kee was getting it for me. One weekend I had to go to school to complete a reading assignment I snuck away with B afterwards. He was back home from offshore and had a room in the North End next to Church's.

I had to rare my seat all the way so no one wouldn't see me. Once we were there, he dressed me in his clothes because a close friend on my momma and daddy side work there at time. We both knew if Netta saw us she was going tell. So, there I was with his big baggy clothes on and a hat to disguise me. Once we were in the room B express that he had falling in love with me. He sung Keith Sweat you may be young but you ready as he undressed me. This was our second time being intimate and it felt like firecrackers going on inside me. He kept telling me your mines and only mines. He was turning me into a woman with every kiss and touch. He knew was on borrow time, so he tried to make it quick and special at the same time. Before he dropped me off, he expressed everything he said he meant and game me enough money to last until he came back from offshore.

Three different times he came pick with me up with Kyle to play it off before BeeBop noticed something going on. That day B, Kyle, Kia, and I went to Lafayette mall. B was mad because I wanted to pick up my pretend boyfriend G-Baby to play it off. He was so upset that he told me I best be lucky Kyle and Kia was there because he would a bust me in the mouth. I guess BeeBop sense that we were having an argument. Boy was in store for an uncomfortable situation. As I sat watching B and them pull off BeeBop told me he knew that I was messing with B and if I didn't mess with him, he would tell Yvette. That night I snuck and called B telling him what BeeBop said. B said he knew that was coming he could tell by the way he was watching you. You have to tell on him he said but how I replied you gone to get in trouble. If I tell he's gone to tell on us. B really wasn't thinking this through clearly. All of sudden a light bulb lite up in my head. I know what I can do I told B. What he asked?

I can put B on my Cousin Lou she'll be down for the count. He said oh yeah that's a good idea. The next morning BeeBop brushed against me in the kitchen asking me if I thought about what he said. I then responded that I would put him on Lou. To my surprise he agreed with it like I thought he would or at least he pretended to. Lou ended up coming spend a night liked planned but they didn't have a chance to do anything. Once she left, he told me he didn't want her he wanted me pinning me to the wall trying to kiss on me while my little Cousin Sweet Pea yelled for him to stop. I moved my face from side to side until he let me go. He through a shoe in Sweet Pea chest making him cry. It was time to tell someone this fool was trying to force his self on me at this point. Not to mentation even my daddy oldest cousin got on drugs and tried to push himself on me as well. It was time to speak up now. When Momo Wanda came home from missing in action for a few days I told her what had took place.

She didn't doubt that it did one bit. She told me she caught him staring at me one night while I was sleeping thinking she wasn't there. She said we had to tell Yvette first thing in the morning while BeeBop was offshore but to our surprise he had done ask her to marry him. Dam it my Momo said this will crush her now. Let's wait she said. So, we waited till finally my Momo was like it's time we can't hold it from her. Just as I thought though Yvette kicked him out the house but was stressing losing her hair and wasn't sleeping. Plus, she still was sneaking and being with him after knowing what he done from Sweet Pea, Momo Wanda, and I. A few days later B was in a bad wreck I overheard someone telling Yvette about it. She had done took my phone, so I had missed all the phone calls from Kyle. When I got to school Kyle had a phone for me that her day brought the day before his wreck.

I immediately called his phone his momma answered and handed him the phone. I saw your daddy he told me. My momma said I was unconscious yelling I'm sorry Bird for messing with Kay. He explained his momma also knew our secret. After I hung up the phone, I called my Momo Cindy to come get me. Telling her how Yvette was treating me and how she whipped me with an extension card bruising my legs. I had tried to get away by spending day over by Quana house with her two daughter Sha Sha and Shira to get away from her. They also knew B and I secret. My Momo Cindy sent my Uncle Carlton and Uncle Chuck to come get me. While putting my things in the car Yvette lied to them about me only wanting to go there to have sex saying I had an odor when my cycle was on recently.

When she knew, she had started hiding the pads from me, so I had to use tissue. Which cause me to have a smell because I kept bleeding through. I was tired of her treating me harshly in front people and always trying to embarrass me when in public. Yes, I wanted to be with B more, but I wanted to get away from her as well. I knew I could sneak off and see him at my Momo Cindy so that too made me want to leave even more. Yvette said she was still keeping my phone when I left but I didn't care B was going to get me another one. So, who cared I said to myself as we drove off? B and I snuck around for three more months after me moving back to Sunset by my Momo Cindy house. By this time his sisters and even my momma knew of our relationship. His sister Erykah was now Bob baby momma.

When B was released from the hospital his momma had gambled all his money he had saved. He had to go back to hustling and he finally noticed that he had to let me go because he couldn't take care of me like he used to. He told me to move on with my life. It wasn't easy I cried and cried and even moved in with my Paron in Lafayette to shake the hurt. My Paron couldn't figure out why I always stayed in my room and never went to events at school.

Not knowing I was healing from the breakup. My Paron kids started to come over more and that kind of took me out that depression state. My Paron was a character himself always doing things to make others

70

laugh. One time we were all in the kitchen eating and he betted that he could eat his whole sandwich at one time stuffing the whole thing down his throat until he threw up. Man, we must a died laughing. The family felt like how it used to be again we was all getting together going on road trips to the beach and living our best of life. Until my Uncle Chuck, Latifah, and Snoop got on the wet cigarettes. After the episode of my Uncle Chuck filling his basket up with things, he thought all was $1 in his basket due to him smoking that stuff. Got to the register and everything was almost $200.

He argued the woman down that he gave her enough and started taking the bags out the store. My Paron girlfriend, Melda, and I had to go get my Paron to come help us explain to my Uncle Chuck he didn't have enough because the lady was getting ready to call the cops. My Paron jumped out the van begging the lady not to call the cops that he would pay the difference. At this point I couldn't breathe from laughing so hard. My Paron blood pressure was rising not only did we almost go to jail before we got to the beach. But Bob had caught a ticket on the way to the beach and didn't have a license. We went a few more times until my Paron finally threw in the towel after Snoop and Bob got in the fight and Bob bit Snoop on the nipple.

That day Bob and Rosey left they kids on the beach and didn't notice until they were on the highway. "That's the last time I ever go somewhere with them again," my Paron said. My Momo Cindy never came because she used that time that we were gone to herself. She was growing tired of always having a house full. She had to do damn near everything by herself wearing herself out. That's why every chance I got I would wash all the clothes and clean up for her. She had done caught 2 strokes and now had high blood pressure from carrying the whole family on her back. She didn't deserve to be living like that and I was feeling hurt because I couldn't take it all away from her. Not only the kids she raised wasn't doing anything with their life but was also stealing from her. Her one-bedroom apartment that was meant for only her now hold over 8 people in it besides her. It was then that I promise myself that I didn't want to be that way. If anybody did something for me I would do back unto them in return.

Chapter Eight
Thug Love

Out of nowhere Deedy hit me up on Facebook. I hadn't seen or talk to him since third grade. Third Grade year Deedy was expelled from school from him humping on me even though I was pushing him from behind me in line he still proceed. The teacher caught him and sent him and Green Eye to the Principal's office. We talked on the phone for weeks until finally my Paron agreed that he could come spend Thanksgiving with us. Everyone took a liking to him, and he started coming around to all our family events. On my seventeenth birthday I moved in with him, his grandmother, uncle, brother, and cousins.

Our relationship wasn't the same when I moved in. I now seen that Deedy was a drug dealer and a certified thug and had been that way for years. Deedy had a hard life as well his momma died when he was only 2 and his cousin that he looked to as a father figure OG had died as well. His grandmother had raised him just like mines did. He started staying out weeks at a time. His cousins Co and Ke kept telling me I was stupid for just sitting in the house while he was out doing God knows what. Deedy didn't want me pretty much going anywhere when he wasn't home. He flashed a few times because of me leaving with his cousins. We would walk from the Trash Pile to the Hill and then to the South Side. Slippers, Nina, Co, Kee, Temp, and myself always rolled deep when I could sneak off. Slippers and I went all the way back to South Street days and Co and I went back to OJ. I was new to the other girls. I remembered Ke, Co sister a little bit from the bus rides to OJ but she was much older than me.

The whole time we were together we would joce and they always clowned about getting me back home for Deedy f***** me up. Temp was dating my cousin Kia, so she was going to through the motions too. When we weren't walking from hood to hood, we would joce in their grandmother house. I dropped out of school in the tenth grade trying to keep up with Deedy after one of his flings was bold enough to call my phone. Kia other girlfriend Al must of of gave her my number. I had met her before on my sevententh birthday when we all went to the moves. I heard through other people that he was messing with Shon but just brushed it off because I stayed with him. I was the main chick, and she was the side piece.

So, the minute she called my phone I gave the phone to Deedy letting him know that I knew about her. Deedy asked, "Who's this?" Once she told him who she was he went crazy. Saying b**** didn't I tell you I had a girl what the f*** you doing calling my girl phone. Whatever she was trying to say he wasn't gone for it because he hung up the phone. He quickly went into the kitchen before I could say anything and told Ke and Co to beat Shon up that she had called my phone. They both caming in the phone talking about now that h** is definitely out of line for that one wait until we catch her. I now knew that my own cousin Kia was allowing them to go to his house like I thought. I couldn't wait to get on the Hill to let him have it. As soon as we all walked up to Kia house this time Deedy was with us. I told Kia since you are letting Deedy sneak with Shon over here why don't you tell Temp you still messing with Al. "Oh yeah," Temp screamed! Kia totally ignored her and swung on me starting a fist fight between us.

Next thing you know he took something off they. fence and hit me with it. I ran in the house and went tell his momma, Lee. Everybody was dyeing laughing outside when Lee and I came back as she told him keep his damn hands to his self. Kia and I was second cousin two sister kids' children. It hurt me because we were so close hell all my fights at OJ was because of him. After that incident Deedy took me trap with him every night. He taught me who was who and who not to ever mess with because they had AIDS. I was a full-time pot head and Deedy taught me how to roll saying don't ever let nobody else but me roll that other people could slip something on me.

When we were out and about, I held his dope and money just in case the cops ran up on him. His grandmother, Ms. Rose, even said one time that was the longest Deedy stayed out of jail. She told him boy that girl is your angel you bet to treat her right. Ms. Rose and I had grown a bond from me always being at home with her when the others were gone. Deedy reminded me so much of my daddy the way he protected me and cared for me. I didn't know how strongly he felt until NeNe, one of his ex's, tried to fight me and he push me to the side and told her he would knock her out if she touched. 'Kia was even shocked by it. Pretty soon the whole Hill knew that I was Deedy girl, and they bet not f*** with me or he was going all out.

When Kia, Deedy, and I wasn't rambling the streets we were watch Boosie new movie Ghetto Stories back-to-back. When things were good, they were sweet but when it was sour it was hell on Earth. That year of us being together consisted of domestic violence, verbal abuse, cheating, many restless nights, and me afraid of something happening to him. Deedy had put his hands on me a few times even pushed me in front of an 18-wheeler before, but I never loved nobody the way I loved him.

I was his first real girlfriend and only girl he ever took home. He taught me the game and gave me love I never had before but could be so evil at times. Me knowing his mother wasn't around to teach him how to love a woman was the reason I held on to him tightly. Especially when my three-month-old sister died in a wreck he was there. That day darn near my whole family was in that wreck but my sister and my Momo Cindy were in the worst conditions. They had to drill holes in my grandmother head leaving her to have learn how to speak and walk all over again. She was never the same after that. I cried like a baby on Deedy shoulders while he caressed my head rubbing it so gently.

I was taking my sister's death hard because my momma was supposed to drop her to me that day. Deedy had turned my phone off due to me getting a phone call from Deon. Tiff brother who was in jail at the time. I periodically talked to him now due to me being in a relationship with Deedy. Deedy grab my phone and answered it wanting to know who was calling my phone. Lord why did he have to call while he was here, I screamed in my head. To my surprise they knew each other and Deedy told Deon no disrespect, but I don't want Kay talking to you. Even though he was making a complete fool out of me he was very jealous and feared of me doing that to him. Deon must have said OKAY or alright because the minute Deedy hung the phone up he slapped the taste out my mouth. As I pulled myself to get up from laying under him, he yanked me back down saying lay your ass back down where the hell you think you going. I told you stop playing with me. Ms. Rose heard the lick and came in telling him I know you not in here hitting on that girl Donnie, calling him by his government name. He told her no man you tripping she didn't believe him one bit. She turned the light on and asked if I was okay, I sucked up the tears and told her yes ma'am I'm fine. Before she turned the light off, she looked at Deedy and said boy God gone to get you for treating that girl that way. Go head Momo he said as she left out.

That night Deedy held on to me like his life depended on it as we slept. That was his sign of apology because his pride never let him. God why I love this boy so much I questioned. I felt one with him no matter what he done or didn't do I love the hell out of him and felt it in my soul. We went on like that for months having or good and bad days. Until one day I just was feed up with him putting his hands on me and me not hitting back. That night we were arguing over him cheating on me. All the stressing and back and forth caused me to lose all my weight and even lost hair over it. Oh, but that night he dived on me I use all my might and kicked him off me into the dresser. He was so shocked that he drew his gun out on me and pinned me to the wall saying I'll kill you bitch! I wasn't afraid not one bit the commotion caused his brother Woody to walk in. Once he saw the gun in my face, he immediately grabs Deedy telling him you are tripping man.

Deedy left out the room hollering if you don't leave tonight, I'm bringing one of my other girls here. His grandmother said no the hell you not and Kay you don't have to go nowhere. Deedy you can go he turn back saying really Momo you are taking up for her. You wrong Donnie she said. I immediately grab my phone and called B and Kyle to come pick me up. I finally had enough. Deedy grandmother of course loved me just as much as him and begged me to stay but I knew that this had went far enough.

Even though he hurt me I still loved him and still went over to be with after I moved out. It was awkward by B because he had a woman living with him and the way she acted you could tell she knew something happened between us, but B constantly told me no matter what his doors was always opened. That summer B was shot by a known jacker from the hood. Even though he saw it coming he was still caught slipping. What hurt the most is that his girlfriend convened him I had something to do with it. I ended up going back to my grandmother in Sunset. That income tax I let Snoop carry me so that I can have enough money to get me an apartment right off Market St. by the health unit. Deedy and I still was going back and forth. I even supported him and went to his court dates with him showing him that no matter what my loyalty for him still stands. After he was still sneaking around on me only this time I started cheating as well.

He had stop putting his hands on me at this point because now he knew I would fight back. I ended up losing the apartment because I couldn't find a job to keep up with the rent. Opelousas was literally maybe 6 blocks. If you ever found a job you had to know someone to get in. So, I kept my clothes and personal items to Bob new girlfriend Rosey house and went stay back with Deedy. At this point I stopped messing with Casey because I didn't want to disrespect Deedy. Yet he still was doing him telling me I was his number 1 and the other girls meant nothing to him. It sounded good but I grew tired if it and moved right back to Sunset. The judge ended up giving him juvenile life due to him catching another charge while still fighting another. My life changed tremendously after he went to jail. I got a job at Popeye's and was now popping bars. I started dating other people but still whenever Deedy needed or called, I was there.

Never missing a beat or letter. I went through a few flings until I hooked up with Face. We hit it off hard and was very close. You see him you see me but that didn't stop him from making a fool of me every chance he got. He also had a problem with his hands. This was another back-and-forth relationship I endured. I was just making eighteen and he was knocking on thirty. I was staying with his cousin Slippers who was also like my cousin. His Aunt Iris and my momma was best friends. Plus, my mom dated his daddy for a good while. So, we all knew each other really well. I ended up working at the Popeye's down there. While I was at work Face was driving my car. My family was pissed and didn't like it one bit saying he was using me. Behind my back he was messing with all type of women. Including my daddy old fling Ronnie. Had me looking stupid in the streets. Even messing with a chick that stayed 1 apartment down from Slipper's house.

But like to die when I started messing with Jay. Snoop homeboy that I had met in Stallion's one night. Then later ran into him on my way from T. Harris. It liked we was destined to mess around because after the club we didn't link up. We started talking over the phone and I discovered that he was married but he told me he wasn't happy. Soon as Face got a whiff that we were messing around, and that Slippers knew and was letting it go on all Hell broke loose. As the boys was outside shooting dice Jay pulled up and handed me his bag with his game in it saying he would be right back to stay the night. One of the boys ended up calling Face letting him know Jay was there. Jay hadn't been back for 10 minutes and in busted D'wana, my daddy sister, telling him that they were outside planning on jacking him. Jay was fresh out of jail. You could tell from his lean cut body and the brightness of his complexation. Jay had long dreads to his mid back.

Reminded me of Biggs off Shottas. As I called Slippers Jay was on his phone with his homeboy Winnie Boo telling him to spray this b**** down I immediately told Slippers get here now. She was at Knuckles house at the time Slippers said "Tuzin tell him please don't do that I'm on my way right now Knuckles come on man." After Jay hung up with him, he called Fred Lamb due to him running the whole North End at the time and most of them on the porch was his boys. Slippers nerves was so bad she sent the laws to run the boys away so a murder scene wouldn't take place. As the laws left Slippers pulled up following behind Winnie Boo and Fred Lamb. Jay explained what happened and Fred Lamb said Face was tripping that he was at chick house right there right now. Fred called Face to come out the house and Jay started saying say Face wassam. Slippers and I pled with Fred not to let them fight. He told us he wasn't gone to let them fight telling the boys to squash the beef and bump fist.

They did and everything was back calm. Jay gave me money to help Slippers out with bills and everything was going great until my two cousins Lou and Tee brought his wife to Slipper's house. Brit Brat and I was sitting outside chilling when they pulled up. Tee jumped out the car bumping her gums, so I called Yvette telling her to get her cousin as they talked on the phone I politely sat back down because his wife was still sitting in the car not saying nothing. Brit Brat had done sent a text to Nita letting her know what was going on. While Tee was on the phone with Yvette Jay's wife Ray finally stepped out the car so say attempting to charge my way and that's when Brit Brat and I stood up letting them know it was up from this point. Lou and Tee eyes widen when they saw Nita 'swangin' coming up the street. Let her go I told the chick that was also with them. Nah she said it isn't bout to be none of that. Well what ya'll brought her over here for in the first place I started saying stepping down off the stomp. It's whatever with me I said, and Brit Brat said, me to. They jumped back in the car and Ray started screaming he isn't gone to never leave his kids as they drove away. Brit Brat and I looked at each other and bust out laughing as Nita pulled up. Nita said all that and ya'll didn't bang man they some amateurs she said.

Call me if ya'll need me she said as she pulled off. Not even 10 minutes later Jay pulled up. I then told him that until he gets a divorce, I don't have time for that bull crap. He said he understood that it was cool, but he still loved me. I ended up going right back to Face and brought my first car from this cat name Nunnie. Face still had never changed like he said messing with girls that was coming over to his momma right under my nose and even with this chick named Peanut that pretended to be my friend. When I found out that he was sleeping around so close to home I lost it and went in on him in front everybody. I had never hit him before until that day. Hell, I was so hurt I tried to hit him with my car. My daddy homeboy BG stopped me from hitting him with the car saying it wasn't worth it.

Once again, I was taken for granted and played on. I ended up moving back in with my Paron in Carencro. I started working a night shift at Walmart slowly getting myself back together again. My Papi passed away and my Paron had gave me his car in trade of mines. I fixed the car up and even put some bang in it. Messing around with the wrong people and started back taking the bars I ended up wrecking the car. Once again, I was betrayed by someone, I thought was my friend, Ronnie. By this time, I was tired of the street life. When my nineteenth birthday came around, I knew it was time for a change.

After locking myself in the room for a month not speaking or talking to anyone the idea of leaving for Job Corp came over my mind. I immediately called and register. Within two weeks I was on the Grey Hound to a better future. Once there I learned who was for me and who wasn't. Out of sight out of mind came crashing down on me. The only people that wrote or looked out for me was my big cousin Josh, Tiff, and Jack. Josh kept me motivated and told me keep going don't quiet up until he caught a murder charge and was sentenced for manslaughter. I was devasted why now when I needed him the most I thought. I continued my journey through Job Corp like he would a wanted. Later meeting a guy named Wendell. The first day in line for lunch he asked me for my number and my crazy tail reply with GO the number 2 Hell.

We both must have died laughing. I ended up giving him my real number and next thing you know we was window hopping. We got close quickly and when Christmas break came, I went with him meet his family in Thibodaux instead of going home to my family. To my surprise his family was really a big family that believed in all coming together. I had never witness nothing like it in a long time. His father was in a biker's club, and they were throwing a Christmas Ball. It turned out nice and everybody had a great time including me that was so tipsy I fell down in their hallway. Only to notice the next day my cycle came on and went off the very same day. We need to get a pregnancy test I told Wendell and to both of our surprise I was pregnant. Boy did everything change within us.

Chapter Nine
How the Dice Roll

It wasn't until I had my first child that everything made sense to me. It linked the chains together for me. Put the missing pieces of the puzzle together. Suddenly, I knew why I went through everything that I went through. Why I saw the things that I had to see. Because of everything that happened, I knew and was well aware of how to raise my son. I took the lessons my grandmother taught me 10 years before to be a better person and a better woman.

The moment I found out that I was pregnant with my son, I knew I had to give him a better life than I had. The first thing I thought of was to marry his father and become a family. Not knowing at the time that everything doesn't always go as planned. Also, that time reveals how people really are. I once heard Steve Harvey say that within six months of knowing someone, they will start to show you who they really are, Even Mya Angelou stated that "When someone shows you who they are the first time, believe them."

Growing up, I always thought that if someone sees how much you love them, then they would change from their wicked and selfish ways and love you back with that same love. Time and time again that theory proved me wrong. And even though I knew the stove was hot, I still touched it, just to watch my hand burn. The very moment my son's father found out I was pregnant he changed. I should have seen that coming from a mile away if I would have been paying attention to the signs. The signs are always there but we just choose to ignore them.

Truth be told, I had a few loves before him. Especially my first real love that was doing a juvenile life sentence in jail at the time. Yeah, you read that right— juvenile life sentence. You see, I was born to love thugs. Hell, my father was a bonified OG up until the day the guy from California shot him. But him being the strong soldier that he was, he fought nearly two years before he took his final rest. I always thought that if only he wasn't taken from me at the age of 14, that my life would have been different. Sometimes I even wished I was adopted by some rich white folks that could give me my heart desires but, dreams and wishes like that rarely get answered in the ghetto.

Wendell blamed me saying I trapped him that he wasn't ready and me being so gullible didn't pay attention to signs still let him come stay with me by my Paron house once I was done with Job Corp. Deedy was released from the detention home around the time and wanted us to get back together even though I was pregnant. Wendell went through my phone and read the texts he sent and ended up calling Deedy. As I was walking in the room from my shower all I heard was Deedy saying boy that's my baby and my girl you got me fucked up and hung up. That's all it took for Wendell to start bugging out again and even trying to cheat on me with a girl that he worked with. I got to sneak off two times to meet up with Deedy before he was kilt. When I found out I was devasted. I kept thinking what if I would 've just went back to him like I wanted to maybe that would a never happened.

Wendell ended up going back home when he found out that he wasn't stopping me from going to the funeral. There I was saying goodbye to the love of my life something in me died that day I saw him lying there. I just couldn't let go he was the first boy's name I tatted on my body. I told him all my secrets and there he was taking every one of them with him to the grave. I thought I had time to circle back around to him, but I didn't. I'll never forget you I whispered as I touched his cold hands. After the funeral I kept having dreams about Deedy that felt so real he called me on the phone in one dream. We talked for a good minute then he said he had to go because his momma was calling him. I told my grandmother she said it meant he was finally with his momma and he came to tell me bye. weeks later I ended up moving with Wendell and his family to get ready to have our baby boy. I named him after his father and nick named him DeeDa after Deedy. Once our son was born, he really started to show his real true colors.

Long story short I ended up leaving my son's father. I moved back to Lake Charles with my Auntie Sally and momma. That didn't last more than two months because like typical black families, instead of them helping you in your time of need, they make you feel uncomfortable and even talk about you badly to others. But me being the person I was, I took my losses. I then moved in with my uncle's wife. That was nothing new to me; I moved from pillow to post all of my childhood life from my grandmother, to my Paron, to my Uncle Carlton, and even to my daddy's sister, Yvette's house. But only this time it was my son and I. After that day, I vowed to get on my feet and get my own house so that my son would never have to go from pillow to post like I had to.

I didn't have a normal delivery, I had to have a c-section, and according to the doctor I had to wait up to six months to start back working. I didn't care what that doctor said, all I knew was I had to make a way for my son. So, I took a job at Cash Magic in Iowa when my son was barely three months old. I had to quit breastfeeding him and give him formula. I was determined to get us our own home. Three months later, the housing authority called with an available two-bedroom one-bathroom apartment. I was so eager and ready to move in that I didn't notice until I had paid my deposit and first month's rent that I didn't have a lick of furniture or house supplies. But I didn't let that get me down, I called a taxi and went straight to the loan company with my son in tow. It wasn't until then that I noticed needed to learn how to prep bottles because my son, DeeDa, was screaming in Walmart. I wanted to break down so badly, but I was determined to get household items from the store. Then later, at the furniture store, I explained to the manager I was a single mother with nothing and before you knew it, he came back saying Ms. Dargin go straight to your home we will be there in 20 minutes.

Once tax season came around, I got a nice little white four-4 door car, which at the time I didn't know they had ripped me off on the price. I got a deal that had me owing 3x more than what the car was worth.

It all went by so fast; From me quitting my job, to enrolling in school, to meeting June. I had never in life been through so much verbal and physical abuse in my life. I lost everything: weight, my car, my focus, my part-time job, and even quit school when I was 1 semester away from finishing. How could I let a man have that much control over me? I didn't know. I couldn't even recognize myself in the mirror. I watched everything I had worked so hard for come crashing down. If it wasn't the different women confronting me, it was him saying the meanest, hateful and ugliest things to me. Something wasn't right about him I knew it. If only I had listened to that gut feeling saying don't mess with him.

Not only did I endured fights with him but also had fights with his mistresses. June was the type that mess with women for the things they had. Then, sweet talk them out they money. I should a known it would be trouble when his first baby momma sent his daughter to come knock to my door saying he took her momma income tax check. While him and his cousin was shooting dice in my front room. I opened up the door wide enough for him to see who was at the door and allowed him to step out and handle the situation. His cousin Lil Kenneth told me that they were lying she gave him the money so, I let that one slide. Not even one month later here comes another one of his baby momma's pulling up behind us while getting weed saying he had her money as well.

At this point I was really puzzled because back home I never saw or heard of any women in our family giving up their income tax checks. Boy did women started to come out the wood works. What took the life out of me was when I saw a flick of him and another chick in his phone. When I confronted him about it, he flipped it around on me. Breaking my phone yelling and calling me all kind of disrespectful names. Like it was me he caught instead. That day I had reached my limit. I told him to leave my house multiple times but instead he went on and on about how nobody would want me, how I wasn't shit without him, and so on. All I remember was blacking out and throwing a full can of air freshener at him striking him dead between the eyes. Blood was gushing everywhere. His reflex made him grab me and for a moment I braced myself for his reaction but all he done was let me go and screamed bitch take me to the hospital. A crack nasal bone and seven stitches still didn't make him none.

The very next day while I went home to take me a bath and change clothes, he had another chick that he was messing with at his momma when I pulled back up. I politely walked clean in the house to the room we were just sleeping in and there he was with her laying on him as he was laying down. All I remember is walking up to him and punching him right in between his eyes busting his stiches right back open. The girl jumped up and blood started rolling down his face. By this time his mom and step daddy heard him hollering and came in the room. See they was knocked on the sofa from the legal weed they had just smoked and didn't see me walk in. As we tussled, I told the girl move out the way this has nothing to do with you. You owe me no explanation but no she just had to say let me at her I been waiting for her.

When I heard those words, I quickly turned away from beating June and started tagging her. My mother-in-law plead with me to take it outside. I had done came out my shirt tagging her. My adrenaline was rushing to the point I grabbed their old skool fruit bowl to pop her with it. June screamed grab it from her quick Ron she's gone to hit her with it for real. His step daddy then grabbed me saying Kay you too good for this just leave him alone as he gave me his shirt. I then turned to Lanna, the girl he was with, and said come outside. When I noticed she was afraid to come outside I started stabbing her tires with a knife. While she looked out the screen door. My mother-in-law was then pushing her out her house saying she had to go that I was her daughter-in-law. Lanna asked my mother-in-law how she couldn't go anywhere with her tires on the flat. Meanwhile, my momma called me screaming Kay bring your ass here before you go your ass to jail. As my Uncle Rusty hollered in the background that's my niece that's what I'm talking about, and a mother fucker better not touch you either. Next thing you know June was on the run for not registering as a sex offender that he never informed me he had to do in the first place. Our whole relationship was based on lies and I didn't understand what type of hold he had on me. I had never been this low before. I was damn near ninety pounds by now. Still trying to hold on to him. We hide out by my momma house until his mother informed the cops where we were. To make matters even worse I found out that he was on the down low. That was the final blow and final straw I could take. How could he just destroy me like that?

I had to go back to my roots, my hometown, just to remember who I was and where I came from. I was back to square one and one month later found out I was pregnant again. When I was just starting to get it together and, was enrolled back in school. Curtis would let me use his car while he was at work to move around. I found out I was pregnant because we both missed work and school that day and decided to go to urgent care to get a doctor's excuse. To make matters worse, my mom had gotten my son taken by his father and I couldn't do anything about it because he was on his birth certificate. Right after June got locked up my mother told my son daddy lies about June messing with little children to keep my son away. When the truth was, he was 18 years old when he got caught messing with a 16years old girl. My life was in a whirlwind and the last thing I wanted to hear was that I was pregnant.

I was afraid to tell Curtis because I knew it wasn't

his; we'd only been together for a month, and I was already past four weeks. I knew he wasn't going to understand. You see, Curtis had been after me since I was 17 years old, working at Popeye's, and the farthest, we got back then was conversation. I couldn't hide it though. I was a truthful soul, and it was eating at me. I waited until I dropped him off at work and made it to school to tell him. Just like I thought, he blew up and told me to bring his car back to him now. I could tell he was furious by the way he was walking when I got there. I simply sat on the passenger side in silence. I didn't utter much of anything because even though a week prior he had told me that he didn't have feelings the way I did for him. But I knew he was lying, and I also knew he had a mean streak in him. So, I just let him get it out. He cursed me out saying I could have just told him I wanted a baby.

Instead of dropping me at my homegirl house, he dropped me at Yvette's house while screaming, "You had a whole baby on me!" thinking that I cheated on him.

He barely let me even close the door before he burnt rubber, speeding off. I burst into tears. How could this be happening to me?

Chapter Ten
Unfinished Business

Later, that day, I called a very good friend of mine, one who has always kept my secrets.

Soon as he picked up, he heard the pain in my voice and said, "Where you at? I'm on my way."

He was 3x my age but was always there for me, so I looked up to him. As soon as I got in the car, I told him I needed $350, and I needed a ride to Baton Rouge in the morning. He saw the pregnant glow in my face and told me, "Kay, before you go through with this, let me tell you a story. My girl and I went through what you about to do and 22 years later, it still haunts me. I never told a soul and neither did she. Oh, if I could take it back, I would. She's had complications with her births since then. I still often wonder what he could and would have been like if we would have had him."

As I listened, I heard the pain in his voice, and I contemplated if I wanted to hold that same burden in my heart. He then took me to get a bite to eat and gave me a little Mary Jane to clear my head before he dropped me off.

I stayed in the house for a month in a depressive state. Why me Lord? My son is only 1 years old, and I can't take care of him right now. I tried to take my mind off of it and work at Shoe Show, but the pregnancy was much different than my first. I couldn't finish my shifts. Meanwhile,

through all of this, my daddy's side of the family was trying to reason with DeeDa's father before things got ugly. Once his father got whiff that I was having another baby, he used it against me. Saying I didn't care about my son. Making me feel even lower than what I already felt. Just me knowing I didn't have a place of my own made me grow in disgust of myself.

Finally, my son returned after his godfather spoke his last words and told my baby father, he had by the end of that weekend to have my son back to me. I was so happy that my son returned, but once he did, he just wouldn't stop crying. I didn't know what made him keep crying like that. I had to play music every night just to make him go to sleep.

We all know how some folks are when they welcome you in to stay in their home, then start acting funny and talking about you to others. While we was staying with Yvette people was telling me how she talked about me having to stay with her.

God had a reason for bringing me back home though. Doing my fair share of going from pillow to post, I learned my baby uncle, more like my big brother, was diagnosed with something he couldn't get rid of. He did promise to hold on until I had Kay'Sha, and I promised to stay home this time to take care of him. But that didn't go as planned. About five months into my pregnancy, he took very ill and told me he was tired and couldn't do it anymore. Of course, I ignored it and told him he had to pull through to hold my hand when I go into labor. My personal diary, my go-to person, my other half was gone a few weeks later and a piece of me died with him. I must have smoked a whole ounce of Mary Jane the day of his funeral.

I know many of you are thinking, How could you do that while you were pregnant? But truth be told, that's the only way I could hold a meal down and ease my mind just enough not to have a miscarriage. You see, I had lost too many loved ones that I held dearly to my heart year after year. My father, my first love Deedy, my baby sister, my Papi, my Aunt Myra, Aunt Jezzy, and Aunt Madge. Every funeral I went to, a piece of me died with them and I found myself not knowing who I was anymore. Just living life without a purpose or a cause. I laid down day in and day out, only coming out to eat, use the bathroom, and take a shower after my uncle past. I had to get it right is what I was thinking and after three months of doing that the thought of moving back to Lake Charles played out in my head.

Situations and phases had turned me heartless by then. Of course, I wanted Quincy to be her father because we grew up together. A relationship that was hard to break, no matter how many years went by. When I got back home, he was the first person I ran to. 15 years of playing hide and go get and momma's and daddies had me wondering what I was missing. You know me being me saw a future with him. Let's just say some people are only meant for a season.

I knew I couldn't dwell on my mishaps because I was only three months away from having my baby and yet had not even a pamper to provide for her. Still, until this day I don't know what it was that led my heart to express the way I was feeling on Facebook, but I did. Immediately after, I received an inbox from a man named Rodney telling me he was related to me on my daddy's side and whatever my baby needed, to let him know and he will ship it to my address. I sent him my paron address, whom I was now living with again, but I didn't believe that he would go through with it.

Throughout my entire life, people made promises, saying that they would be there in a time of need, and how I could always call on them, but they were never around or wouldn't commit to their promises made. Time and time again they let me down or agreed to help just to criticize and talk badly about having to help me. I always had to get it how I lived. It wasn't until he started sending me screenshots of everything that, he was buying for her and the dates to expect them that I believed it was true. For two weeks straight, packages were coming in. Kay'Sha had everything she needed to where I didn't even have to have a baby shower.

He was one of the main reasons that made me truly believe that there were good people here on Earth. That in fact everyone wasn't just there to laugh and make fun of you in your time of need, but some people would help with a sincere heart. From that point on, Rodney and I had a very tight bond. We talk all of the time, uplifting one another and just being a listening ear when either one of us needed to vent. It was like we grew up together vs just getting to know each other.

To be honest, I only knew of my daddy's immediate family because my grandmother wouldn't let them near me. Not to be ugly, but to protect me from seeing too much at an early age. But once I reach a certain age, she allowed me to go because she knew it was hurting me not to know the unknown. Like I said before until I was eight years old, I thought Maxwell the artist was my father. For years her and my daddy's mother went at one another's necks behind me not going around them. Even though my grandmother knew the lifestyle my father's side of the family was living she never once talked badly about them or told me otherwise why I couldn't go. I had to find out as I aged why she tried to keep me away.

The blessing from Rodney made me feel like I could go on and not have to worry anymore. He promised that anytime I needed anything, I could count on him. And every time I did need him, he was right there, time after time.

Finally, I was feeling like myself again.

Immediately after having Kay'Sha, I moved back to Lake Charles. Me living the fast life had me testing two men to be my daughter's father, even though I knew in the back of my head that June was her father. The man that messed my life up. So many thoughts were going through my head. I ended up appling for college again and the Sunday right before my semester started, I got a call that my favorite Cousin Kia was killed. Talking about a blow that knocked the life out of me. Revenge and retaliation played through my head day in and day out. How we were raised and the things we saw played a huge role in the outcome of our lives and the choices we chose but, it was here and now that I notice it was time to get it right. My little cousin didn't make it to see twenty-five years old. I learned a huge lesson that the streets were killing us off, one by one and to make matters even worse it was us killing one another. Black on Black crimes. Kia said he wouldn't stop until he was with Deedy, and guess what he was laid to rest right next to hm.

As I said my goodbyes, I made a promise that I was going to do it the right way for all of my family that was resting in peace that didn't get a chance to make it out. It felt like it just wouldn't end because not even a month later I had to watch my daddy's other first cousin bury his son. Was our family cursed is all I kept asking? I never in a million years would have thought I would have lost so many loved ones. Many questioned how I didn't lose my mind. Truth is, I went along like they were still here, but I just can't physically see them anymore. My daughter opened my soft spot again and made me love myself and my life again. I stop moving fast and stuck with my goals until the end.

One month after starting school, I moved into my own project with nothing but our clothes, an air mattress, and a fan. I remember like it was yesterday, my baby girl was screaming her lungs out because it was so hot. I slowly furnish my project. Day in and day out, I walked my kids to daycare and walked to school. Carrying my son on my back and my baby girl in her carrier in the front. Talking about rough times, many nights I laid in my bed with my kids crying, begging God to help me because this time I was trying, and I wasn't going to stop until I made it right. I wanted everything that I knew I deserved. Hell, all of the stuff I went through and been through I was not giving up.

I never did have support or help, so at this point, it didn't bother me much. For almost a year and a half, my life went on like that. One day, a lady picked me up and gave me a ride. After we dropped my kids at daycare, she turned around and said, "Baby I don't know you but, I just want you to know I have been in your shoes before, keep on pushing. This too shall pass."

The school I was going to was stealing our finical aid and robbing us blind, but still, I said I wasn't quitting. I started making friends and they would take turns picking my babies and me up. I gave them money for gas. I was a single mother of two on welfare and food stamps. Still, to this day I don't know how I managed.

While in school, I had a few flings but nothing major, or no one that saw the vision that I saw. I had made up my mind that I wasn't settling anymore. I didn't have time for games anymore nor time to waste on any man. I had lost too many loved ones to the grim ripper to care if a relationship didn't make it. I rolled on.

When I met Keithen that was the beginning of an even clearer vision. He became my best friend, always saying uplifting words to me. Telling me how I was the strongest Black woman he had ever met. At this point, I started noticing that once you have your mind made up to do good and reach higher heights, doors began to open up and the right people are there waiting on the other side. All of my life I believed I didn't need anyone because I never had anyone there, but the truth is everyone needs someone. I was at the point that I was going after success, and I wasn't going to stop until it was mine.

Always remember if you get anything out of life you had to put up with the toils and strife. Meaning no matter what you go through or what comes your way, you can't fold under pressure. Only the strong survive. Always believe and know the rain doesn't last forever and the sun must shine sooner or later. Everything happens for a reason and there's always a lesson to be learned. You could never know too much.

Let's just say I witness my fair share of changes that came along to test me. My last semester into school I ended up hooking up with this old skool guy from around the way named Bell. That's when the roller coaster ride began. Not from him but from the women he had before his encounter with me. Many had something to say because he was forty and I was twenty-three. Talking about a big age difference. It was just this one baby momma of his that just went too far, and she just so happened to come around at the humblest time in my life. Now don't get me wrong, I was never the one to pick or cause mess. It took a whole lot for me to come out of character.

Growing up many underestimated my humbleness.

It was a few times I had to stand up and let them know what I was capable of, little or not. Win, lose or draw I was gone get the respect I deserved.

The thing that irritated me the most was that his baby momma liked to damage others' belongs but was a coward- bully. Throwing rocks and hiding her hand. I went through damn near eight tires in two months. Cops were getting called to my place of residence where my kids laid their heads. Talking about mad disrespectful.

On top of that, I received a call from my little sister saying they hadn't seen or heard from our mother in two weeks and that CPS was going to take them if I didn't come to get them. So, of course, me being me, I took in all three of my siblings when not another soul didn't even bother. Our whole family knew the situation but only wanted another topic to talk about. Now here I was with my dude crazy stalking baby momma, my momma's three kids, plus my two, but remember like I said there's always a lesson to be learned.

This baby momma of his was out to destroy everything I had worked so hard for. She went so far as to putting a fake criminal charge against me. See when you are going through the whirlwind you can't see why. The only thing that saved me from catching a real case was I knew one wrong move would cost me custody of my brother and sisters, plus a record that would prevent me from pursuing my career. At the age of twenty-three, I had no record, and it was going to stay that way. I hired a lawyer and went to court to fight the case and won. Leaving with no assault charge and having to take one anger management class. Thanks to my English teacher Mr. Guillory.

Even though I had already graduated college with a 3.8 GPA I still wasn't joyful.

The school that I had given two years of my life

to wouldn't give us a proper graduation to let our kids see our success. The only good thing was that I had landed a job at Habitat for Humanity, the company I did my internship with. I started off with ten dollars an hour as a finical assistant. The projects that we had moved into was a wreck, not just the neighborhood, but my household itself. If it wasn't my two sisters and brother, it was Bell and me at each other neck from the drama with his baby momma. The whole time I didn't know it was teaching me how to cope under pressure.

My daughter's father was even playing a role in it. See June knew firsthand what I was capable of because he saw that side of me that didn't understand or knew what humble was. He knew firsthand that I used to be a ticking time bomb from the fights with him and his mistresses. So, he thought that was what it would be like with this situation, but I knew this time around I had too much class to even be bothered with unlikely breeds. I came too far to be a two-time loser.

My brother ended up going to the detention home for breaking into cars. Meanwhile, my little sister, MumPatty, was rebelling against everything I said. They never had rules and boundaries enforced the way I enforced them when they lived with my momma. Even though they were my siblings, I treated them as my children. So, whatever I felt and knew I wanted my kids to have and not to do, and to be and not be, I was trying to install into them. My sister didn't see it that way though, so she asked CPS to remove her from my home. My heart was so heavy, but I couldn't show it because I knew it was something, she had to go through on her own to figure it out.

Things were really going down heel with me and Bell and I found myself going back to my old habits. Then there came T, my elementary school crush. One late night riding through my hometown, Opelousas, I decided to hit the scene and check out The Back— a very popular late night after the club spot. Bingo! There he was. You see, I'm a rare breed, I never allowed a man to pick that he wanted to be with me. Nah, it wasn't easy like that. I would watch my opponent for years without them even knowing it. Watching the way, they moved. I was raised in a house with five uncles, what do you expect? Did I have a poor sense of judgment… hell yeah, I did. Mostly going for the roughnecks and pure thugs.

I knew if I stared at him long enough that, he would get that feeling that someone was watching him. Boom! Just as I thought, the eye contact started. I lingered around for a few more minutes, then I bounced. I got so far as the next street and my body was calling for me to turn around to go get what's mine. When I pulled back up, I notice the dude he was with outside. I called him to my car from the window. I could tell from the look on his face he thought I wanted him. Sike! I looked up at him and said, "Hey, where old boy you were with at?

In the midst of asking him, T peeked his head out the door. T's homeboy face dropped as he said let me go get him for you. Just as I thought, T was bold just like me. He walked up to my window and said, "What's up?"

"What's up with you? I replayed.

After five minutes of talking, he jumped into the passenger seat of my car, and it was up from there. When I said I was going back to my old habits earlier, I meant I hadn't even broken things off with Bell yet. I was the type of person who felt I didn't owe an explanation to anyone. If I feel something isn't right, I just go with it. Things weren't right with us and hadn't been for months. As I played Space Age Pimpin' by 8ball & MJG T said, "man that's my type of music." "You're messing with me or not?" he asked. I replied yes and in return he leaned over and gave me the juiciest French kiss. He then told me to drop him to his truck and follow him while he dropped his homeboy off. I followed and that night we made love felt like our souls was one. Even when T told me he was married, it felt like it was meant to be. Actually, I knew for a fact that it was.

We both went with our moves not caring about what was at stake. I started going to my hometown every weekend spending all of my free time that I had with him and only him. It then got to the point that I wasn't even sleeping with Bell. Especially when I moved my family out the hood and into a subdivision in Welsh. Yes, I said ME. I paid all of my bills and all Bell ever did then was take care of my hair, nails, and money to blow. Now don't get me wrong he took care and feed the whole family while I was in school until I was capable to do it myself.

Even though I didn't say anything about T, he wasn't dumb. He knew there was someone else, but he wanted me to tell him and that's something I just felt like I didn't owe nothing to him. T and I were so caught up that he was making sure he was landing jobs that were close by or staying at hotels in Lake Charles so I wouldn't have to drive all of the way to him. We couldn't stay away from each other. Soon everyone in our hometown knew what was up. We were more than lovers we were best friends. It wasn't until T had gotten to the point where he started to get very territorial that I noticed thing were getting serious. Many times, we said this was our last time but we both knew it was a lie. All it took was for us to see each other or for him to get a whiff that I was in town.

My Momo Cindy always said that the same thing that makes you laugh will make you cry. One night, I went by his sister's house to get my hair done. T and I were beefing at the time, or should I say going through the spell of us knowing we were wrong because he was already spoken for. He was married with one son already, plus a baby on the way.

Every day I questioned how I could let myself go this far. A one-night stand turned into months of passion and love with the quickness, but T always claimed that he had things under control. Even though my gut feeling told me not to believe that I did anyway. Should have known it when he blocked my car in by his sister's house, telling her she bet not touch my hair in the front of her clients, whom one was his wife's cousin. His sister tried to calm him down but once that oil is in T's system, it doesn't matter what you say, he's going to do what he wants to do. Even I knew alcohol makes a man show his true colors. That night he cursed me out low as a dog because he thought I was going to meet another man when I was trying to go to the Yamblee Building. His sister literally had to kick him out of her house to stop him.

She called me to the back and told me that was his wife's cousin, and that T shouldn't have done that. T's sister and I went way back since middle school.

T was waiting for me outside. I already knew how this was going to turn out. Just like every other episode ending with me not going anywhere but with him. This time was different though and I felt it. It was time for me to tell him bye, but how? Especially when I struck him with my car and burst his lip, I knew then it was time.

That Sunday night his number kept calling and hanging up until finally I said, "T what the hell you got going on?"

He screamed, "It's not me, it's my wife!"

At this point in life, I felt untouchable. I was making

eighteen dollars an hour at work and had been promoted within four months of being there to Family Service Coordinator. So, T knew, and I knew I could take care of myself. Yeah, it would hurt like hell, but our time had run its course.

That night, T was supposed to tell me in front of his wife that he was going to leave me alone, but he couldn't fix his lips to say it. The next morning the wifey finally called herself to figure out what was going on, and of course, remind me of how low down and dirty I was for messing with her husband. No doubt, I knew I was, but that feeling we shared was too strong and real to not risk it. The truth was that when we were together it was like he was mine and I was his, but you know in this world there's always a time to grow up and realize life doesn't always give you what you think is right for you. I already knew her cousin went back and told her what took place that night. All she wanted was my word that I was going to leave him alone and after I called him a few times afterward to say my mends, it was over. Goodbye, T.

It wasn't easy for me, I had to wing myself from the vibe I got used to with him. I couldn't let it get me too down. I had to put my big girl drawls on and keep it pushing. I beat myself up for it for over five months, wondering how I could allow myself to feel so strongly for him. Hell, it felt like God put us here just for each other, but how could that be when he said vows with someone else?

I made a promise to myself that no matter what I would never do that to myself again.

Not only did I lose my lover, but I lost my best friend. Damn T.

To Be Continued